"Why did you help me? You could've walked away. Left me there."

"No, I couldn't have," he said.

"Sure you could. It would've been easy. My body would've been found eventually and no one would be the wiser that there was someone who could've saved my life." She stared at him for a long moment without saying another word. "Something tells me you know how to cover your tracks, so there must've been some reason."

"You're welcome for saving your life," he said, debating whether or not he should tell her everything. She needed to know that her fall had been no accident. "Now that you're up and around, I'll drop you off in town tonight."

"And then what? You'll disappear?" she asked.

She shouldn't care what happened to him because she needed to be concerned about herself.

"Don't worry about me," he said.

"Too late for that."

SUDDEN SETUP

USA TODAY Bestselling Author

BARB HAN

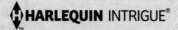

HARLEQUIN INTRIGUE®

Many thanks to Allison Lyons, the absolute best editor. My enduring gratitude to Jill Marsal, the absolute best agent. I'm privileged to work with both of you and count my blessings every day.

Brandon, Jacob and Tori, nothing in my life would make sense without the three of you. Your smiles bring joy and light to every day. Bitty Bug—our fairy-light chats are the highlight of every evening.

Babe, how lucky am I? You make me laugh, lift me up when I cry and cheer me on every single day. If I could be granted one wish, it would be that every person could have this kind of love. I can only imagine how much better the world would be for it. I love you.

PLEASE RECYCLE

THIS PRODUCT IS RECYCLABLE

Recycling programs for this product may not exist in your area.

ISBN-13: 978-1-335-52629-8

Sudden Setup

Copyright © 2018 by Barb Han

HARLEQUIN®

™ www.Harlequin.com

Printed in U.S.A.

USA TODAY bestselling author **Barb Han** lives in north Texas with her very own hero-worthy husband, three beautiful children, a spunky golden retriever/standard poodle mix and too many books in her to-read pile. In her downtime, she plays video games and spends much of her time on or around a basketball court. She loves interacting with readers and is grateful for their support. You can reach her at barbhan.com.

Books by Barb Han

Harlequin Intrigue

Crisis: Cattle Barge

Sudden Setup

Cattlemen Crime Club

Stockyard Snatching
Delivering Justice
One Tough Texan
Texas-Sized Trouble
Texas Witness
Texas Showdown

Mason Ridge

Texas Prey
Texas Takedown
Texas Hunt
Texan's Baby

The Campbells of Creek Bend

Witness Protection
Gut Instinct
Hard Target

Rancher Rescue

Harlequin Intrigue Noir

Atomic Beauty

Visit the Author Profile page at Harlequin.com.

CAST OF CHARACTERS

Ella Butler—This heir to the Butler fortune took an almost deadly fall while hiking Devil's Lid. But nothing about what happened that morning was an accident.

Holden Crawford—This man has a past that could kill him and anyone who gets close to him.

Sheriff Clarence Sawmill—This sheriff might be in over his head with a high-profile murder to solve and a town in chaos.

Ed Staples—This Butler family lawyer works behind the scenes to keep the family going no matter what.

Maverick Mike Butler—Even in death this self-made Texas rancher has a few cards left to play.

Andrea Caldwell—Does this girlfriend have murderous intent?

Troy Alderant—This land developer is trying to buy Mr. Suffolk's land but at what price?

Rose Naples—This well-meaning friend is going out on a limb that could easily snap in two.

Mr. Suffolk—When this land owner's shotgun turns out to be the murder weapon, his son steps up to claim responsibility.

Chapter One

Whoever said mistakes don't define a person didn't have a clue. Holden Crawford stood over the petite woman curled in his bed, figuring that helping her would cost him dearly. He shook his head at his own stupidity. She'd already been in and out of sleep for a day and a half, and he was beginning to worry that she'd taken a harder knock to the head than he initially assessed. As soon as she woke and he made sure she was all right, he'd drive her close to the sheriff's office. Then he'd disappear. Again.

Holden had recognized Ella Butler immediately when he saw her hiking. She was the daughter of the wealthiest man in Cattle Barge, Texas—a man who was helping Holden out while he needed a hand and a protected place to stay off the grid.

His daughter was trouble times ten. His best bet would be to leave her in the cabin with a few supplies and take off before anyone connected the dots that he'd been there. And yet, abandoning her while she was so vulnerable wasn't something he could do. Even someone as hardened as him couldn't walk away like this.

Holden ignored the annoying voice in his head that tried to convince him sticking around might be an option. His duffel was already packed and sitting next to the door.

He'd told himself that staring at the wavy-haired beauty as she hiked along Devil's Lid was for survival reasons and not because those long, silky legs of hers were highlighted perfectly in pale pink running shorts. He'd needed to see if she would detour to the cabin on the outskirts of her father's property where he stayed and expose his hiding spot. Hell, it had been his sanctuary.

Out of nowhere, her head had snapped to one side and then she'd lost her footing. She'd free-fallen a good ten feet before hitting the hard clay soil. She'd rolled another twenty before meeting an equally rough landing at the bottom of the gulch.

It had been no accident.

At that point, Holden had had two choices: help or walk away. Tracking the responsible party hadn't been a serious consideration, although Holden didn't doubt his own skills. It was more important to make sure she was safe first. But there was a problem with helping her.

Ella Butler was news.

If it hadn't been ninety-five degrees at eight o'clock in the morning, he would've cleaned her wound and then left her with a couple of water bottles for when she woke. August weather was too unforgiving to leave her stranded and the gash on her head was serious. Holden had had no choice but to bring her back to the cabin.

To complicate matters, she'd blinked up at him. He had to know if she remembered him when she woke because if she could give his description to law enforcement, the real trouble would begin.

Holden walked another circle around the room.

Questions ate at him. First of which, what kind of fool hiked alone in one of the most remote and barren places of the Butler property? There were all kinds of dangerous creatures out there, and he should know because he'd found a scorpion in his boot yesterday morning and had crossed paths with a coral snake by lunch. He recalled the childhood saying he'd been taught to tell the difference between a coral and a harmless snake with similar markings: *red on yellow, kill a fellow; red on black, venom lack.* This part of the country had no shortage of venomous creatures.

There were other concerns about leaving her alone. Did she know there was no ready water supply? He'd had to hike for miles to locate a decent place to dig to find the lifesaving liquid when he first arrived. Making the trek had become part of his daily routine after morning push-ups and was the reason he'd seen her in the first place. His daily schedule had been the dividing line between life and death for Ella Butler.

Holden had kept an eye on her to ensure that she didn't get too close to his camp. The place sat on the westernmost boundary of the Butler property referred to as Tierra del Fuego, meaning *land of fire* in Spanish.

If he was being completely honest, he'd admit to being intrigued by Ella. He'd chalked it up to too many days without female companionship and his dread at realizing the time had come to move on from Cattle Barge.

He'd spent a little more than two years on the run. Two years of not speaking to another person. Two years of eating every meal by himself without anyone to share his life with. And yet in a strange way, Holden had felt alone his entire life.

Scouting a new location was a lot of work, but his diligence had kept him alive so far. He'd been on the move twenty-five consecutive months, never pausing for more than a pair of weeks in one spot. This was the longest he'd stayed in one place, and his instincts had told him that it was time to go even before he'd witnessed the assault.

The problem was that he liked Cattle Barge. Holden felt an unexplainable connection to the land. He'd let his emotions win over logic in staying on too long. He'd erred by not listening to his instincts. And there'd be a price to pay for that lapse in judgment, he thought as he looked down at her.

ELLA'S EYES BURNED as harsh light and a sharp pain in that spot right in the center of her forehead, like a brain freeze, nailed her. She blinked a few times, trying to clear the blur. The outline of a very large man looming over her came into focus, causing very real fear to surge through her. Ella tried to force herself awake but darkness pulled. Her mind screamed to get up and run. Her limbs couldn't comply and so no matter how hard she fought against it, her eyes closed and she gave in to sleep.

It was dark by the time Ella woke again. She vaguely remembered being helped outside to go to the bathroom once, or maybe it was twice, but then she might've dreamed the whole episode.

Glancing around, she tried to get her bearings. Her head pounded as she strained to figure out where she was. The bed was hard but comfortable. There was a blanket draped over her. It was clean and soft.

Instincts kicked in and she felt around to make sure she had clothes on. Movement sent shards of pain needling through her skin. A flicker of relief washed over her when she realized her shirt and shorts were on. The respite was short-lived. Her eyes were beginning to adjust to the darkness when she saw the silhouette of a man folded forward in a chair in the corner. Based on his steady breathing, she surmised that he was asleep.

Ella couldn't make out his face from across the room but a warning buzz shot through her at the

sheer size of him. Questions raced through her mind
but she couldn't bring one into focus. Exhaustion
kicked in again and it felt like she'd run a marathon
in the August Texas heat. All she could do was close
her eyes and rest. So she did.

"What time is it?" Ella asked, unsure how long
she'd dozed. She'd been awake for a few minutes,
assessing whether or not it was safe to talk. The sun
was up. Her thoughts had been engaged in a battle
of good versus evil, debating the intentions of the
stranger in the room. Eventually, logic won out. If
this man had wanted to hurt her, he could've done
so already. Still, she'd walk a fine line with him and
make sure she didn't provoke him.

"You're asking the wrong question," the strong
male voice said—a voice that sent electric chills up
her back.

"What should I be asking then?" She tried to push
up to sit but her arms were too weak. The male figure made no move to help her.

"It's Thursday." He turned his back to her in a
surprising show of trust and picked up whatever was
on his plate. He popped something into his mouth.
It must be what smelled so amazing. Her stomach
growled despite being convinced that she wasn't hungry.

She scanned the room for anything she could use
as a weapon while he wasn't watching. Her vision
was improving even though looking around still

made her eyes hurt. She glanced at the door, hoping to find a baseball bat or something she could use if push came to shove. There had to be one around there somewhere, her head would argue because it felt like one had been used to crack it open.

The room was sparse. There was the makeshift bed in the corner that she was presently resting on. A very uncomfortable-looking lawn chair—the one he'd slept on last night—was pushed up to a table, which was nothing more than a piece of drift board propped up by stick legs tied off by rope. Either this guy was a survivalist or a former Boy Scout. She couldn't decide which one.

Ella remembered that the stranger had slept hunched forward on that chair made of lightweight aluminum and cheap material. Only a gentleman would give up his bed…right?

Embarrassment heated her cheeks as she recalled him helping her outside to use the bathroom. If he'd wanted to take advantage of her, he'd had plenty of opportunity. And yet he wasn't being welcoming.

The plate the stranger ate from was some kind of metal, like she'd used for camping with her brothers and sister when they were old enough to set up a tent in the backyard. It had come in an outdoorsman kit, she remembered.

She performed a mental calculation that took longer than it should have and made her brain pound against her skull. "I've been out for two days?"

"In and out," the stranger said. She didn't recognize his voice at all and she knew she would remember such a deep baritone if she'd heard it before. There was an intense but calming quality and it sent a trill of awareness through her, which was totally inappropriate and unwelcomed. She chalked her reaction up to hitting her head too hard.

"I'm sorry, have we met before?" she asked, hoping to place him. Her mind was fuzzy and she was having a hard time processing information.

"No."

"Then can I ask who you are?" Ella racked her brain trying to figure out who he could be.

"No." There was finality to his tone that sent a different kind of shiver down her spine, an icy chill that said he was a man with secrets.

The thought of being alone with a person who wouldn't identify himself made Ella want to curl into a ball to protect herself. Her father was one of the richest men in Cattle Barge, Texas, and her life had turned upside down after being given the news of his death a few days ago. When she really thought about it, this man could be after her father's money. She was still fuzzy as to why she was here in the first place, and no matter how hard she tried she couldn't come up with a good explanation. She'd lost more than the last two days because she didn't even remember why she'd gone hiking in the first place.

And then it hit her. Had she been abducted?

"Good luck if you're trying to get ransom for me from my brothers," she said. "My father was killed and all of our money is tied up right now."

"I'm not interested," he said, his voice a low rumble. He froze.

If it wasn't ransom money he was after...then what?

Ella didn't want to go there with the physical thing. Besides, there was something strange in his voice when she'd mentioned that her father had been killed. He'd stopped what he was doing, too.

"I should go." She tried to force herself up on weak arms.

"That's not a good idea."

Icy fingers gripped her spine at his response.

"I'm perfectly capable of getting up and walking out of here and you can't stop me," she said with more indignation than she'd intended. It was the latent Irishwoman in her. Her mother had had the bright red hair to match, or so Ella had been told. Dear Mother had disappeared when Ella was too young to remember her and had never looked back. Ella took after her father with his honey-wheat locks and blue eyes. She had the stubbornness to match. She was also astute, and it didn't take a rocket scientist to realize the stranger was hiding from something or someone. And now she was alone in a cabin with him.

She had no plans to let her guard down.

"You need to hydrate. You wouldn't make it a mile in this heat in your present condition," he said.

"Do you live here?" she asked. He seemed to know the area pretty darn well and he was right. She wouldn't last long in the August heat without provisions.

All he did was grunt in response.

Ella looked around, trying to find clues as to who the mystery man could be. The place was tidy. There was no dust on the floor. Her gaze slid to the door where a makeshift broom was positioned. It had been made from hay that had been tied together at the base of a tree limb. Whoever this mystery man was, he'd set up shop with the intention of sticking around awhile. He had survival skills, too. Her mind immediately headed down a negative path… Who would want to be alone on the most remote area of her father's land? *A man who has something to hide*, a little voice answered. He could be a doomsday prepper, bank robber or—gasp—serial killer.

Her gaze darted around in an effort to find evidence as to which one he was.

To the other side of the doorway sat a duffel bag that had been zipped closed. She fought against her worst fears that there were torture instruments in there.

The stranger turned around and she could barely make out his features for all the facial hair. His build was football player big and he had to weigh in at well over two hundred pounds. He was pure muscle and his size was intimidating. That thought sent a trill of awareness skittering across her skin. Under different circumstances, she could appreciate the athletic grace with which he moved. Ella's five-foot-five-inch frame was no match for this guy. Working the ranch kept her strong and in shape but she was small by comparison.

The lawn chair scraped against the hardwood flooring, drawing her attention.

"You didn't tell me your name," she said.

Another grunt came in response as the large figure moved toward the bed. Ella scrambled backward—pain shooting through her with every movement—until her back was against the wall. She fisted her hands, ready to swing if he gave her any indication that his intentions had changed.

There was something in his hand as he moved toward her, the light to his back. His sheer size blocked out the sun rays coming from the window and bathed her in darkness. Her body was ironing board rigid.

"Be still. And relax. I'm not going to hurt you," he said, and he looked offended as his features came into focus.

"If that's true, why won't you tell me your name?" she asked, not ready to trust him.

"You're better off not knowing." His side was turned to her and his face was partially hidden. He didn't make eye contact. Up close, she could see that he would be quite attractive if he cleaned up that beard or shaved it off altogether. More than attractive, actually, she thought as her stomach did an inappropriate little flip when he turned and she could really see into his eyes.

The man was clearly hiding something and an attraction was so out of the question that she had to choke back a laugh. Her emotions were all over the map. How hard had she hit her head?

"I'll be the judge of that," she said, seeing how far she could push her luck.

The layer of blankets dipped where he sat.

Her heart pounded in her chest and it felt like there was glue in her mouth for how dry her tongue was. Her entire body was strung tight.

"Let me see that gash on your forehead," he said in his deep baritone. It had an amaretto-over-vanilla-ice-cream feeling and had that same warming effect on her insides. This close, she could see that he had deep-set, serious eyes that were the lightest, most pure shade of blue that she'd ever seen. A square jaw was covered by that dark beard. He had thick, curly hair the shade of a dark cup of coffee.

"What happened to me?" She inched toward him, not ready to give much more.

"I'm a man of my word. I already told you that I wouldn't hurt you and I won't. So move a little faster, will you." He sounded frustrated and impatient.

"Well, excuse me if I don't jump into the arms of

a complete stranger when he beckons," she snapped back. Talking made her skull hurt. Could her brain be in actual pain? Speaking of which, now that blood was returning to her limbs, her entire body was screaming at her.

A smirk lifted the corner of the stranger's mouth. He quickly reeled it in.

"I have two pain relievers in my hand if you'll sit up and take them," he said, holding out his flat palm.

Okay, so he wasn't lying about the twin tablets. But who knew if they were OTC or not.

"What are those?" she asked.

"Ibuprofen," he stated. His tone was about as flat as stale beer.

She stared at them like they were bombs about to detonate.

"There's a bottle of water on the floor," he said, leaning toward her.

She let out a yelp that caused his entire face to frown.

"I've already said that I won't hurt you. I brought pain relievers and a wet napkin to clean some of the dried blood from your forehead so I can get a look at your injury. I didn't do it before because I didn't want you to wake with a stranger standing over you." He shot her a look of aggravation.

That actually made a lot of sense and was considerate when she really thought about it. She wasn't exactly ready to relax because he could still be a weirdo, and she was too weak to put up much of a fight. Besides, what was with the secrets? Sharing his name would go a long way toward winning her trust. Instead, he acted like a criminal. If he wasn't one, he needed to come clean.

"I'd apologize personally if I knew your name," she said, matching his level of irritation. He wasn't the only one who could be frustrated.

"What were you doing out here all alone?" the stranger asked.

"I don't know," she responded. If he wouldn't give out any information, neither would she.

He shot her a look that cut right through her.

"I was hiking. I must've lost my footing and hit my head," Ella said, pressing her fingertips to her temples. "It's all still a little fuzzy."

Brooding pale blue eyes examined her and she saw the dark circles cradling them. Whoever this guy was, he had a lot on his mind. There was something else there, too, but she didn't want to analyze it because it made awareness electrify her nerve endings. It also made her aware that if she'd been asleep for two days she must look like a train wreck and have breath that could wilt a flower.

Blue Eyes dabbed the wet cloth on her forehead above her right temple. She winced.

He muttered a curse and pulled his hand back. "That hurt. I'm sorry."

"It's okay." Why was she reassuring him? Reason

took over, reminding her that he seemed intent on helping her. She was in a vulnerable state and while she couldn't exactly trust him, she also had no reason to think he had plans to hurt her.

He gave her an apologetic look.

"Best as I can remember, I was hiking pretty far out on the trail. Most of how I ended up here is fuzzy. Am I allowed to ask what you were doing out there?" Ella flinched again when the cold, wet cloth touched her skin.

"No more questions," Blue Eyes said. He made a move to stand.

Ella caught his elbow.

"Please don't leave. My father was killed and that's the last thing I remember. I have no idea what happened or how I got here. I'm not trying to be a jerk, but I've just been told that I've been out of it for two days. I have a gash on my head that I don't even know how it got there, and I'm so thirsty I could suck a cactus dry, and despite that, I really need to go to the bathroom," Ella said, letting all the words gush out at once like a geyser whose time to erupt had come.

"Can you manage on your own?" He motioned toward the door and there was a storm brewing behind those blue eyes at the mention of her father.

"I believe so," she said.

"Toothbrush and toothpaste are on the sink. Bathroom's outside." He turned and walked out.

Chapter Two

Holden needed air. He lifted his face to the sun. The Texas heat beat down on his exposed skin, warming him. Maverick Mike was dead?

For a split second Holden feared that he could be the reason, that the men who were after him had somehow connected him to his father's friend. But that was impossible.

This was a wake-up call. Helping Ella had been a knee-jerk reaction and Holden could feel himself sliding down a slippery slope with nothing solid to grab hold of. He owed her father for offering him a place to stay when Holden was at a low point, and that was the reason he'd told himself that he stepped in with Ella. Speaking of her father, the news still hadn't quite absorbed. Holden rubbed his chin through the overgrown scruff. How could Butler be gone?

The door opened and Ella froze as soon as she saw him standing there.

"I'll give you privacy," he mumbled. Someone needed to toss him a lifeline because the woman stirred feelings he hadn't allowed in longer than he could remember—feelings he never wanted to experience again. Then there was the obvious fact that he couldn't afford those feelings. They'd have him wanting to stick around and protect Ella Butler while they figured out who wanted to kill her. Holden reminded himself that he'd done his part. He'd kept her alive.

"Why did you help me? You could've walked away. Left me there. No one would've known any different." She positioned her hands on either side of the doorjamb.

"No, I couldn't have." He made a move toward the door to indicate that he was done talking. She didn't flinch.

"Sure you could. It would've been easy. My body would've been found eventually and no one would be the wiser that there was someone who could've saved my life." She stared at him for a long moment without saying another word. "Something tells me you know how to cover your tracks, so there must've been some reason."

"You're welcome for saving your life," he said, debating whether or not he should tell her everything. She needed to know that her fall had been no accident, but he'd keep the part about his connection to her father to himself. "Now that you're up and around, I'll drop you off in town tonight."

"And then what? You'll disappear?" Her gaze zeroed in.

She shouldn't care what happened to him because she needed to be concerned about herself.

"Don't worry about me," he said.

"Too late for that." She issued another pause while staring at him. There was something about her cornflower blue eyes that he couldn't afford to notice. "I'd like to properly thank you for what you've done to save my life. Any chance I can convince you to come back to the main house with me?"

"Sweetheart, I've been taking care of myself for a long time. I really don't need—"

"Obviously, you need a place to stay." She glanced around as if for emphasis. "We're always looking for a good pair of hands around the ranch. It's clear to me that you'd make a good addition and we need more men like you."

"You ought to be careful who you go offering jobs to," he stated.

"I trust you."

"That's a mistake," he said plainly.

"No, it isn't. But even if it was, it wouldn't be my last." One of her balled fists was on her hip now. She had a lot of sass for someone in such a vulnerable position. He'd give her that.

This conversation was going nowhere so Holden did what he did best: went silent as he stared her down. She should be more afraid of him than she was acting. She had been earlier when she'd opened her eyes, and as much as he didn't like it at first, her reaction was for the best. What had he done to make her so comfortable now?

"You want coffee?" he finally asked, shaking his head. She was as stubborn as the stories he'd heard about her father.

"That would be amazing, actually," she said with a small smile.

"Then get out of my way."

She twisted her mouth in a frown at his sharp tone but stepped aside. He walked straight past her without making eye contact even though she stood there expectantly for minutes afterward. And then she slammed the door shut. Not only was Ella stubborn but she had a temper. The nuances of her personality were none of his business. Period.

Holden refocused on the facts. Ella Butler had been missing for two days. His position at the cabin had been compromised from the moment he'd witnessed the attack, and he could see now that it was a miracle no one had shown up. The situation was declining. Fast.

There'd be a search underway by now. The news that "Maverick" Mike Butler was killed would be enough to create a full-scale media circus in Cattle Barge. Add a missing heiress to the equation and Holden couldn't begin to wrap his mind around how out of control the coverage would be. He'd been so far off the grid that he'd missed all of it.

The news that her father had been murdered before an attempt had been made on her life sat in Holden's gut like he'd eaten a pack of nails. The media attention surrounding her disappearance—and that would be big news—must be the reason the person who'd chucked that rock at her hadn't returned. Holden had been watching out for the culprit.

She needed to know that the blow to her head wasn't an accident. He wasn't sure how she'd react, especially given the fact that she'd just lost her father. Normally, he'd suspect someone close to her, a family member. Money or greed would be motive for murder, and especially when considering the amount Maverick Mike had amassed. His fortune was legendary but so were his antics. He had a lot of enemies. Holden wanted to ask about the circumstances surrounding her father's death but decided against it for the time being. He shouldn't show too much interest in the Butler family. Once he settled into a new location far away from Cattle Barge, he could find out what had happened. Mike Butler's death would be all over the news, so it would be easy to find.

Holden glanced at his watch. Ella had been gone a full ten minutes. Should he check on her?

A thousand thoughts rolled through his head. Adjusting while in action had always been Holden's strong suit. He told himself this time would be no different. The door opened at about the time he'd made up his mind to mount his own search. She looked at him boldly.

"Coffee's getting cold," he snapped. She needed to be afraid. He set her cup on the table that he'd made by hand after he arrived last month. The cabin was the first place he'd bothered to put together anything that resembled furniture. His thinking had always been "get too attached to any one place and leaving would be that much more difficult."

His plans had really gone south in Texas—but then he was beginning to see why the place was so appealing with its wide-open skies and thousands of stars at night.

Ella moved to the table and picked up the tin mug. She cradled it in her hands like it was made of pure gold when she sipped. A little sound of pleasure drew from her lips. "This is really good. How did you do this?"

"You haven't had any for too long. Muddy water would taste good to you right now." Holden kept the part that he liked giving her that small moment of happiness to himself.

"I promise the coffee's not this good at the main house." She paused and then her eyes brightened. "I don't know what I've been thinking. My brothers and sister are probably frantic with worry right now. There's no chance you have a working cell phone, is there?"

"No." He was completely off the grid. There was no way to track him using technology.

"I need to reach them and let them know that I'm okay. I know what I said earlier about our money being tied up, but if you're in some kind of trouble I can help." The determined set to her jaw said she meant it.

Holden shook his head. The less she knew about his circumstance, the better.

"I'm more concerned about you right now," he said. "Besides, you're news and that's bad for me."

"You're on the run from something." She had part of that right.

More like *someone*.

Her gaze penetrated deep into him. "You know who I am, don't you? You've always known."

He nodded.

"And you're not out to hurt me. So far, from what I can tell, you've been helping me," she continued.

"I want you to listen carefully to what I'm about to say. What happened to you out there was no accident," he warned.

She gasped. "Not *you*…"

"No, it wasn't me. But someone did that—" he motioned toward the gash on her head "—on purpose."

He let the revelation sink in for a minute.

"It wasn't you and it wasn't an accident," she said so quietly that he had to strain to hear.

Holden handed her another cup filled with beans

he'd warmed in the fire. "You're used to better food, but this is protein and it'll keep your stomach from growling."

Ella took the offering with trembling hands as his message seemed to be taking seed. "Who would want me dead?"

He didn't like that momentary lost look in her eyes.

"I'm telling you because you're going to want to be careful from now on. Take necessary precautions and don't wander off alone." Holden leaned his hip against the counter.

She took a bite of food and chewed.

"You said that your father was killed," he continued.

"Yes."

"You'll want to look at people who stand to gain from your death after his to start. Scrutinize those closest to you," he said, figuring with her money she could hire proper security who could keep her safe until the law found the man trying to kill her.

"I have no idea. I mean, I think what you're saying is that my brothers or sister might want me dead to get me out of the way or take my share of our inheritance, but I trust them with my life," she said.

"What happened to your father?" he asked. The look he shot her must've been interesting.

"He was shot twelve times while he slept naked

in the spare bedroom attached to his office in the barn," she informed.

"No one heard anything?" he asked, thinking that someone had wanted to make a point. An act like that came across as anger motivated.

"The barn isn't near the main house. Dad liked to keep home and work separate," she said.

"Which is difficult, considering you do live your work when you own a ranch," Holden said. "Your family would know everyone's sleeping patterns and where your father would be on a given day."

"He spent a lot of nights in the barn. What makes you so sure it's one of them? Did you used to work in law enforcement?" She turned the tables.

"No." Holden had no plans to elaborate on his background. The less she knew, the better for both of them.

"We leave as soon as the sun goes down," he said, closing the bag to the coffee grinds.

ELLA REALIZED SHE'D been gripping the coffee mug so tightly that her knuckles were white. She reminded herself to breathe as she tried to absorb the reality that had become her life. Her brothers would not try to hurt her. For one, the Butler kids had had each other's backs since childhood after their mother had taken off and left them with their father. They'd had to. Their father wasn't exactly skilled in the parenting department. He'd loved them in his own way,

Ella thought defensively. She'd always felt the need to protect her father. But he wasn't the problem this time.

Thinking made her brain cramp.

Ella eyed the stranger carefully. By nightfall, she'd be done with him. He'd be out of her life forever. She should be happy about that, and yet the thought tugged at her heart. Maybe it was because she'd lost so much already with her father's death. Or it could be her soft spot for lost causes. There'd been countless stray animals that she'd made space for in the barn only for her father to tell her they had to go. Usually, they were injured and she knew they'd never survive on their own. Her brothers or sister would come to her rescue and help her keep them hidden until she'd manage to nurse them back to health and then find a new home.

A few were worked into the menagerie of pets on the ranch. Oftentimes one of the hired hands would end up with a new pet to take home to his family. And many of the employees at Hereford Ranch covered for her to help with her causes. No one went against Maverick Mike's wishes directly, but everyone pitched in behind the scenes to help Ella.

Looking back, it was probably difficult for them to turn away such a persistent little girl. Ella had been told more than once that she had the campaigning abilities of a politician.

Her gaze drifted to the wounded person standing

before her with no name. If anyone needed to find his way, it was the man across the room. She told herself that was the reason she felt an unexplainable draw toward the mystery man and it had nothing to do with the inappropriate surge of attraction she felt every time she glanced his way.

"What will you do once you drop me off? You can't stay here anymore, can you?" she asked.

"You need to worry about yourself. Use some of that money you have to hire extra security," he snapped.

Ella bristled.

His voice softened when he said, "You're in danger and you owe it to your father to be careful."

"Why do you care?" she asked.

"I don't," he said. "But you should."

A noise sounded outside and Blue Eyes dropped into a crouching position in half a second flat. The remarkable thing was that he made no noise with his movement, and that made her think he might have a military background.

His gaze locked onto hers and the look he shot her warned her to be quiet. She froze, fearing that whoever had tried to kill her was back. Would they have returned to verify that she was dead and then go hunting for her when they didn't find a body?

Her pulse raced.

With effort, she slid off the chair and made herself as small as she could on the floor. Movement hurt despite the couple of pain relievers he'd supplied earlier. Ella knew Blue Eyes had this under control. And it struck her as odd that she felt safe with the stranger.

Thinking about the attempt on her life made her realize that there could be others coming to town to get a piece of her father's will. Hadn't his attorney, Ed Staples, warned that there could be a lot of surprises forthcoming? Even though he couldn't possibly have meant this, Ella was beginning to fear that the actions of her father would haunt her and her siblings long after his death.

When the silence had stretched on for minutes, Blue Eyes moved to the window and checked outside. Without speaking a word, he slipped out the door.

Ella moved to the window to get a look for herself, watching as he moved stealthily. There was a certain grace about him.

Despite his untamed appearance, his muscles gave the impression he maintained a disciplined workout schedule. In fact, looking around the room, it was obvious that he liked things tidy. Something had made him want to drop out of civilization for a while. He couldn't be a doomsday prepper because he seemed to have on hand only what he needed for a couple of days. She wanted to offer him some type of reward for saving her life but he'd already refused work. What else could she do? Offer a reward?

Ella thought about her two brothers, Dade and Dalton, and sister, Cadence. She wasn't kidding before.

They'd be frantic with worry about her by now. Even though her siblings had left town to escape the media circus in Cattle Barge, one of the employees would've contacted them about her disappearance. She'd been out of communication for two days…and with a total stranger. He could've done anything he'd wanted to her. A shiver raced through her. But he hadn't.

For that reason and a few others that she didn't want to overanalyze, Ella intended to figure out who this man was and why he was running.

Chapter Three

Blue Eyes walked back into the cabin, glanced around and then picked up his duffel bag. "Finish your coffee. We're leaving ahead of schedule."

"Everything okay outside?" Ella asked.

He didn't respond.

"Is someone out there?" Her heart rate jumped a few notches higher.

"Not now. There will be," he said and mumbled, "I should've gone a long time ago."

That statement implied he wouldn't have been around to help her and she didn't appreciate the sentiment. "Well, I, for one, am glad you outstayed your welcome. I wouldn't be alive otherwise."

She was getting indignant. She couldn't help herself. He wouldn't tell her anything about himself and she wasn't trying to take advantage of him or turn him in to the FBI. All she wanted to do was find a proper way to thank him. The guy was working her last nerve and her head still pounded.

"Why don't you come to work for me on the ranch?" she asked while watching him pull out bleach wipes from his bag. He wiped down the dishes before placing them inside the duffel. Now he really had her curiosity heightened.

"I already said that I don't need a job." For the irritated sound that came out of his mouth next, she would've thought she'd just asked him to scrub the toilet with his toothbrush.

Ella made a production of glancing around. "Are you being serious?"

He shot her a warning glance. It said to tread lightly.

She ignored it.

"Because as far as I can tell, you very much need a paycheck. And a decent place to sleep." She waved her hand around.

"I had one until you came along and messed it up for me," he quickly countered.

"You can't be serious," she said.

"Try me."

"Is that a threat?" She planted her balled fist on her hip. It was probably the fact that she'd almost been killed that was giving her this new bravado. She didn't care. The guy had some explaining to do and he was squatting on her family's land.

"No. If you haven't figured it out already, I'm try-ing to help you," he said, opening up a knife and cutting the rope he'd used to hold together the table. The metal sparkled in the light. He wiped down each leg.

"Why won't you let me return the favor?" she asked.

Another frustrated noise tore from his throat. "You don't have anything I want."

That sounded personal. She tried not to take offense. "I'd like to offer a financial reward. Surely, you could use some money."

He didn't look up but waved her off.

"At least tell me your name," she persisted. Why was he being so obstinate? Was it really that difficult to give her something? Granted, she was used to getting what she wanted and with enough persistence she was sure that she could wear this guy down, too. She didn't have the luxury of time and she wanted to send a proper thank-you or reward for his help.

"I've already told you that's not a good idea." He broke one of the legs in half and then tossed it into the fireplace.

"I disagree." She stood there, fist planted.

"You always this stubborn when you're wrong?" he asked, breaking the second leg and tossing it on top of the last.

"I'm usually right," she said. Ella glanced around. It wouldn't be dark outside for hours.

"Since you're feeling better, I'll take you to town. Go to the sheriff and tell him what happened. I'd appreciate it if you left me out of your statement.

That's how you can thank me for saving you." Another broken table leg, more tinder for the fireplace.

"I thought we weren't leaving until the sun went down," she said, a moment of panic crushing her. Her father was gone. Nothing at the ranch would be the same without him. She hadn't even begun to deal with his murder. An attempt had been made on her life. Of course she would go to the sheriff but she wasn't quite ready to return to town and the unknown waiting there.

"Plans changed."

"You won't tell me why? I mean, I realize that we heard a noise but everything's okay now, right?" She was still trying to figure out why she was arguing for more time with the man who wouldn't even tell her his name. Logic be damned. Ella needed to know he was going to be all right. At least, that's what she tried to convince herself and not that there was something magnetic about this man that was completely foreign to her.

"Being seen anywhere near you is dangerous for me."

"What have you done wrong?" she asked, figuring she might as well go for it.

"Nothing that concerns you." He broke the final leg and tossed it into the fireplace. She might not understand his way of life but she appreciated his self-sufficiency.

"Then tell me what you're running from," she said in a last-ditch effort to get him to talk.

A moment of silence passed between them as they stared each other down.

Okay, he won. Ella wasn't in a position to bargain and this stranger seemed intent on keeping his secrets. He'd helped her and she was grateful.

"I probably haven't sounded like it so far, but I really do appreciate everything you've done for me," she said as she moved toward him, toward the door.

She paused before crossing over. For a second, time stopped and they just stood there, staring at each other. A sensual shiver goose bumped Ella's arms. The stranger had the most amazing eyes, piercing eyes. Eyes that she could stare into for days. As odd as it sounded even to her, the moment felt intimate.

The attraction she felt caught her completely off guard. Rugged mountain men had never been her type. It was probably the mystery surrounding him that held so much appeal and the fact that all her senses were on full alert.

Ella broke contact as she heard the *whop-whop-whop* of helicopter blades in the distance.

"Let's go," she said.

HOLDEN SAT AT the counter of the diner in neighboring Rio Suerte. Another couple of hours and he'd be out of Texas altogether. He'd dropped off Ella Butler two blocks from the sheriff's office. She could retrieve her Jeep near Devil's Lid once she gave her statement to law enforcement. Ella was smart enough to take it from there. He'd done his part, repaid his debt to Maverick Mike.

Time to move on, he thought with a heavy sigh. He hadn't thought about the murders he'd been accused of for two days while he was with Ella. The initials, HA, hadn't haunted him. He'd discovered them etched into the bottom of a chair leg at his father's place—the chair where his father had been tortured and killed.

Holden shook off the bad memory. He was no closer to figuring out what had happened then he'd been two years ago.

The restaurant was a typical off-the-highway food stop and seemed like the place frequented mostly by truck drivers. Holden had befriended more than his fair share while crossing the country, making his way to Texas. The diner was shaped like a train car. There was one row of booths behind him matched by a long counter with bar stools for single travelers. Two families were in the booths, no doubt stopping off for a quick meal while on a road trip.

There was only one truck driver in the building. Bathrooms were to Holden's left, near the end of the counter where the cash register was located. There was one cook in the kitchen and only one waitress on duty. The cook was significantly shorter than Holden, bald, with thick arms. He bench-pressed.

The man was in his early fifties with a cook's belly. Holden dismissed him as a threat. He fell into the same category as the dads. One drove a minivan, the other a Suburban. Holden could tell they were from the suburbs based on their clothing—one was in jeans and a polo shirt, the other wore warm-ups and a T-shirt. They had that haggard look that came with long road trips with young kids.

The truck driver was substantial in size, mostly fat from spending his days seated. He looked strong, though. Holden could see his arms in the sleeveless flannel shirt he wore. The man couldn't be ignored as a threat. If Holden assigned levels, five being the highest, the dads were ones and the truck driver was a two and a half, maybe three.

There were exactly two exits in the building: the front door he'd come through and the one in the kitchen. Holden was used to memorizing every detail, looking for every possible escape route. Doing so had kept him alive. Was he really living?

Holden dismissed the thought as going too long without human companionship. His brief run-in with Ella Butler reminded him of everything he didn't have. He'd been alone for a very long time, focused on staying alive, staying one step ahead of the men who were after him. They were good. He was the best. And that was precisely the reason he was still breathing.

The waitress approached. Her metal-plated name tag read Deena.

"Make up your mind?" Deena asked, motioning toward the menu. She was in her late thirties and had early wrinkles around her eyes and mouth. Her neck was the biggest giveaway of her age.

"Chicken-fried steak with mashed potatoes and gravy, carrots. More coffee when you have a chance," he said.

She wrote down his order on the ticket with a smile, a nod and a wink. "Sam makes the best."

"I'm counting on it," Holden said, returning the smile. He excused himself to the restroom. He wanted to splash water on his face and wash his hands before he ate. He didn't sleep much while he'd been taking care of Ella.

As he stood in front of the bathroom mirror, he was shocked at the stranger looking back at him. Furry face. Dark circles under his eyes. His thoughts snapped to Ella Butler and her initial reaction to seeing him. No wonder she'd been so afraid when she'd first opened her eyes. Hell, he would be, too.

He pushed those unproductive thoughts aside.

Holden splashed cold water on his face before washing his hands. Maybe it was time to shave the overgrowth. He hardly recognized himself anymore, and he certainly looked more animal than man. It was easy to do while he'd been mostly living off the land. And yet his reflection had caught him off guard.

Walking out of the restroom, he scanned the room. The situation was the same. The threat potential was low. He reclaimed his bar stool and did his level best not to look at the TV mounted in the corner of the room. A cursory glance revealed the channel was set to local news.

Holden picked up his fresh cup of coffee, ignoring the screen. He didn't treat himself to a restaurant meal often. This was a delicacy he had every intention of enjoying.

And then he made the mistake of looking up.

There was a picture of the Butler ranch on the TV screen. The story was about an heiress's life being in danger. Holden gripped the cup and waited...

Another attempt had been made on Ella's life. A witness had seen a man trap a woman between two vehicles on a residential street one block from the sheriff's office. The woman managed to fight off her attacker before slipping around an SUV and disappearing between two houses as at least one shot was fired. The witness, who would only agree to speak anonymously, recognized Ella Butler but was too frightened to get close enough to get a description of the heiress's attacker. There was a lot of blood at the scene and a manhunt was underway for a gunman wearing a ski mask. He was considered dangerous and authorities cautioned people to keep a distance and call law enforcement immediately if he was spotted.

Holden could think of a few other things he'd like to do to the guy besides turn him in.

He released a string of curses under his breath. It was his fault for taking her to town in the first place. He'd left her there without transportation or a way to escape. Damn it. This was on him.

Anger roared through him along with an overdose of guilt.

He listened for any other news about Ella and sighed sharply when he learned she was missing and believed to be injured.

"I need my check," he said to Deena.

Chapter Four

Ella rolled onto her side, ignoring the pain shouting at her. She could feel her pulse pound in her thigh where she'd been shot and pain gripped her in between the temples. She was losing blood, which was not a good sign. At least she'd managed to fight off her attacker and run. She'd poked her fingers through the ski mask he wore and had managed to knock him off balance. Then she'd bolted. It had all happened so fast. The blast. The cold, wet feeling spreading through her thigh.

Who would want to hurt her?

The stranger's warning hadn't been an over-reaction. Her life was in danger. She'd been in such a fog earlier that she hadn't even thought to ask any of the right questions. Could Blue Eyes have identified the rock thrower?

She crawled into the front landscaping of the modest home on Sixth Street, gasping. How long could she stay there unnoticed? A few minutes? Hours? The night?

It was getting late. She'd barely escaped the gunman. If only she'd been able to get a look at his face. And now she was hiding, on the run from someone determined to get her out of the way. She searched her mind for a name, anyone who would want her gone. Could this be related to her father's death? Or was the timing a coincidence?

Her father had enemies and plenty of people didn't like him, but it was as if he'd been made of Teflon and she could scarcely believe that someone had managed to get to him. Her heart fisted and grief shrouded her, weighing down her limbs. Her larger-than-life father was gone. She was hiding in someone's landscaping and she had nowhere to go.

A sob released before she had time to force it back. Tears brimmed but she couldn't allow herself to cry. Not now. Let that dam break and the flood might just leave a trail big enough for her attacker to find her. Start crying and she might not be able to stop.

A branch snapped. She glanced around, afraid to breathe in case the gunman was closing in on her.

Hope that the noise could've been the sheriff or one of his deputies—anyone who could help— fizzled when she saw the bobcat winding through the front landscaping. He was fairly small and definitely not a threat. But it reminded her that there would be others. Soon.

Ella needed a plan. Her thoughts shifted to the compelling stranger in her father's cabin. He was strong enough to defend her. She told herself that was the only reason he entered her thoughts and not because of something deeper, something like missing him. Missing a stranger sounded ridiculous, even to her. How much blood had she lost? She had to be delirious if she was thinking about Blue Eyes.

One thing was certain. If she surfaced in the open, she'd be killed the second her chaser caught sight of her. The shotgun that had been fired at her shot real shells, as evidenced by the blood on the outside of her thigh where shrapnel had grazed her. Speaking of which, she needed to clean her wound before it got infected.

She couldn't go home. There was too much chaos going on since news of her father's murder broke and she'd be an open target.

She had no idea what the person targeting her wanted. Ransom? Revenge?

She and her siblings were close-knit. They'd had to be since it was generally up to the four of them to handle things at home. Their father had been tougher on the twins. She'd been protective of Dade and Dalton when they were young. They'd long since grown into men who could take care of themselves and everyone around them. Ella and the twins had always looked after their younger sister, Cadence.

Speaking of her siblings, she needed to warn them

but had no way to contact them. Thankfully, they were tucked away, far out of town, having left immediately after news broke of their father's murder. They'd decided to get away from Cattle Barge until this whole mess blew over and life returned to normal, whatever that would be now that their father was gone. With his unconventional lifestyle, she and her siblings had feared people would come out of the woodwork to claim stakes in his vast fortune. Based on the traffic she'd seen coming into town and the resulting chaos, the others had been smart to leave. Someone had to stick around and make sure the ranch was still running, and Ella had convinced them it should be her.

But being in town was dangerous. So was the ranch. She didn't suspect any of the workers who'd been around for years. There were a few new hands. She couldn't rule out the team her father had put together even if she doubted he'd put anyone questionable to work on his ranch. He loved his family and was fiercely protective of them even if their relationships with him were highly individual and complicated. He'd never knowingly put them in jeopardy. *Knowingly* might be the key word. Could her father have put his trust in someone who'd duped him?

Her brain hurt. Her body ached. And some of her memories were patchy thanks to the blow she'd taken. At present, she was exhausted, hungry and bleeding. Her mind was going to places that she wouldn't normally consider. She knew exactly where she needed to go so she could take a step back and think this through but had no idea how to get there. Her Jeep was parked near Devil's Lid, which wasn't doing her a lot of good. Blue Eyes had ridden her into town on his motorcycle.

There was no way she could make it to the sheriff's office. The person who was after her could be watching. If she got anywhere near—

A hand clamped over her mouth. Ella gasped. She tried to bite but whoever was behind her was too fast at securing his grip—and it had to be a man. His hand was huge. He'd been stealthy, too. She hadn't heard a peep. Her pulse pounded and adrenaline caused her body to shake.

"Be quiet and I'll get you out of here," said the familiar voice—the voice that belonged to Blue Eyes. "Can you walk?"

Her pulse raced from fear mixed with another shot of adrenaline. She nodded and his other hand slipped around her. A second later, she was being helped to her feet.

"I'm shot," she said and could feel the physical impact of those words. No matter how much Blue Eyes tried to deny he cared about what happened to her, his body language belied his words when his muscles pulled taut with the news.

"How did you find me?" she asked as the initial shock began to wear off while they were on the move.

The motorcycle was parked at the end of a quiet street.

"I saw the news story about the attempt against your life," he responded without missing a beat. "I recognized this area as close to where I dropped you off and tracked you by the blood trail I found."

He made it sound easy but it couldn't have been. How had this stranger become so good at hunting down a person? She decided this wasn't the time to ask. By all accounts he was helping her…but he was so secretive before and it had her imagination churning against all logic. She didn't like the confusing feelings she had toward him.

"How do I know you're not going to hurt me?" she asked.

A frustrated-sounding grunt tore from his throat. "Seriously?"

Now all her defenses flared. "Yes. I'm a woman. I'm injured. Basic survival instincts kick in at some point. I have no idea who you are. I don't even know your name."

"If I wanted to hurt you, I would've already done it." That deep voice reverberated through her, sending a trill of awareness coursing through her. "We've already covered that."

Okay, she could concede that point.

"Who are you?"

"My name is Holden Crawford. Now that you've heard it, forget it as fast as you can. Knowing my name will only end up hurting you more," he said. "That's why I didn't tell you before now. It's not because I'm trying to hide something from you or don't trust you. I haven't had a real conversation with someone in more than two years. So I'm guessing by your reactions to me that I'm pretty bad at it. Can't say I was especially good with idle chitchat before, so…" He shrugged massive shoulders. "And the last person I really cared about ended up dead."

She gasped.

"Not telling you my name has been my way of trying to protect you," he continued. "Your father was good to me, offered to let me stay on his land, and I figured I owed him one for it. That's the reason I helped you and didn't walk away. I'm not that good of a person to stick around for pure reasons. It was a debt. One that has been paid."

"Sounds like you're a better man than you want to admit," she said.

"Me? Nah. I know exactly who I am, what I am, and it's not good for someone like you," he stated. "You're better off without me."

A frustrated grunt tore from her throat.

He turned to face her.

"I'm sorry about that." He glanced at her thigh and a trill of awareness blasted through her, which was unwelcomed. There was something primal and magnetic that pulled her in when she was near Blue Eyes. Sex appeal over standard good looks? "That was my fault, and I came back to make it right."

"You're on the run from something you didn't do."

"That's what I said." He held out a helmet and waited for her to make a decision.

"Maybe I can help you," she offered.

The look on his face said he doubted it.

"It's now or never, sweetheart. The choice is up to you. Go with me and I can't take you to the law."

Ella figured her options were pretty limited at the moment. She had no idea who was after her. Going to the sheriff was logical, but getting there safely wasn't guaranteed and the man who was after her would most likely expect her there. Striking out on her own wasn't even a consideration. She was injured and had none of the necessary skills to survive. Go back to the ranch and she couldn't be certain that she'd be safe.

"Let's go," she said, taking the offering. "And my name is Ella, so you can stop calling me sweetheart."

She slid onto the seat behind him. He took her hands and wrapped them around his chest.

"Hold on," he said, like there was another option.

Ella turned her head and pressed it against his strong back as wind whipped around her.

Adrenaline had long since faded by the time they reached the cabin and exhaustion made it difficult to lift her leg over the motorcycle. Holden helped her take off the helmet and then he secured it to the back of the seat, mumbling something about needing to get another one. Texas didn't require one by law, but most riders seemed smart enough to take the precaution.

Ella stared at his face. Beneath all that wild facial hair was an attractive and capable man, and she ignored what the revelation did to her stomach.

"Did you get a look at who did this to you?" he asked.

"No. He had on a ski mask and it was dark outside, so I couldn't get a good look at his face," she said.

A disgusted look crossed his features. "This is my fault. I shouldn't have left you there and especially not without a vehicle."

She leaned her weight on him as he put his arm around her waist, hoping she'd feel less vulnerable if she knew a little more about the stranger who was helping her. More electricity fizzed through her as he walked her inside the cabin, and the overwhelming feeling that she was safe for now settled over her.

"Sit still," he said as he retrieved a bottle of water and poured it over her thigh. "I have something that'll help with the cut on my bike."

He brought in medical supplies and attended to her wounded leg.

"Who are you *really*?" she asked, staring up at him.

"A man defined by his mistakes." He stepped back but maintained eye contact, holding a second too long. The dark lines of his serious expression said he meant every word of that. Fire shot through her when she realized the implication of what he said.

"You think helping me was a mistake?" She scoffed. Anger had been building and she'd explode if she held it in any longer. "Well, then, I'm sure glad you went against your *superior* judgment or I'd be dead."

"Twice," he said through clenched teeth as he stood. His breath was a mix of mint and coffee. An infuriating part of her wanted to see what that tasted like. He raked his fingers through thick, wavy hair.

"Now that you've saved me again, why not just leave? My Jeep isn't far from here. I'll head north, away from the ranch, until I figure out who's doing this to me," she said with more anger than she'd intended.

He took a threatening step toward her, closing the gap between them even more, and this close she could almost sense what his skin would feel like pressed against hers as she stood.

Ella blew out a frustrated breath. She thought the same curse that he muttered when she said, "Mistakes aren't the only things that define a person."

Holden caught her gaze again and she felt the moment her anger turned to awareness. Awareness of his strong, masculine body so close to hers. Awareness of how much he turned her on even though she fought against it. Awareness of how good it would feel to have his hands on her, roaming her skin.

"Do tell," he said, and there was so much sexual undercurrent running between them.

"We're also defined by our choices," she said.

"Fine. This is one of mine." He dipped his head and kissed her.

His lips, pressed to hers, sent a current of need rippling through her and heat pooled inside her thighs. She'd never been *this* aroused *this* quickly in her life, but then a sexual current had been building between them since she'd first seen him.

He tensed, like he expected her to fight back, but all she could do was surrender to the out-of-control wildfire spreading through her. She stretched her fingers out and smoothed them across his chest as she parted her lips. His tongue dipped inside her mouth and she could feel the groan rumble from deep in his chest.

The realization she was having the same effect on him that he had on her was satisfying. A frustrating and intense sexual draw stronger than anything she'd ever experienced enveloped her. That strength of an emotion could be dangerous. Holden was dangerous.

Instead of pulling back, which would be the most sensible move, Ella wrapped her hands around his neck and deepened the kiss.

His arms looped her waist and he hauled her body against his. She could feel his heart pound inside his chest at a frantic pace. Her breasts strained against her bra as they pressed flush against his muscled chest.

How on earth was it possible to feel so much heat in one kiss?

Holden's strong, flat palm slipped inside her shirt and her nipples pebbled. He hesitated at the snap on her bra and then all of a sudden her breasts were freed. He released a guttural groan as he took one of her full breasts in his hand. He teased the nipple, rolling it between his thumb and forefinger, and her stomach fluttered.

He pulled back long enough to search her eyes. He seemed to need reassurance from her that all of this was okay.

Was it?

Ella didn't want to think. For once, she wanted to go with what her body craved…and right now, that was the blue-eyed stranger.

He pulled back. "See what I'm talking about?"

She studied him.

"I've needed to do that since you woke up the other day," he grumbled. "And it's a huge mistake."

He had that right, she thought, as anger flared through her.

"Don't worry. I'll make sure nothing like it ever happens again," she said.

Chapter Five

Ella could not, under any circumstances, allow Holden Crawford to affect her. She moved away from him and onto the makeshift bed, grateful that he'd left it intact. She needed...something—physical space, maybe—to clear her mind. What she wouldn't do for a strong cup of coffee right now.

"I need to get a message to my family and make sure they're okay. Whoever is doing this to me might also be targeting them," she said, needing to redirect her thoughts and gain control of her overwrought emotions. Her attraction to him could be explained in simple terms. She'd almost been killed. Twice. He'd saved her. Twice. The magnetic pull she felt was nothing more than primal urge.

Holden studied her for a long moment. He had that wrinkled-forehead expression that made her believe he wanted to speak his mind. He seemed to decide better of it.

"Where are the twins and your sister?" he asked.

Ella couldn't mask her surprise. She was going to have to get used to the fact that this stranger knew more about her than she did about him, reminding herself that he was one of her father's many acquaintances. But then, it seemed like everyone knew her father or at least believed they did. She also realized that for all his antics, her father wouldn't help someone who broke the law. Maverick Mike was many things, but he wouldn't harbor a criminal and especially not anywhere near his beloved family or ranch. Despite complicated relationships, family was everything to Maverick Mike. His property was a close second. Her father had loved his land and everything about Texas was sacred to the man. She'd inherited his zest for family, the ranch and her home state.

"I don't know exactly. They disappeared to get away from the media circus surrounding Dad's death and I didn't think to ask," she said. "We all have places we go when we need time away."

"Why did you stick around?" His gaze narrowed and his lips thinned.

"Someone had to stay in order to keep an eye on the business," she stated. "An operation as big as Hereford doesn't run itself."

He gave her a look of concession. "Your brothers didn't see it as their jobs?"

"As a matter of fact, they did," she said, a little indignant. "They wanted to stay but I convinced them that they should take some time away."

"Your arguing skills aren't in question but I'm still surprised they agreed," he said with a shake of his head.

"Well, they put up a good fight. But I managed to convince them." That was putting it lightly. She'd almost had to physically force them off the property.

She looked at Holden, who seemed not to believe her.

"You may not realize it, but I can be pretty convincing when I need to be," she defended.

"On second thought, I shouldn't doubt that you know exactly how to get what you want," he said with a tone she decided to ignore rather than explore. Mostly because it sent more of those unwelcomed shivers up her arms.

"What about you?" she asked, realizing that he wasn't saying more than two words about himself.

He didn't answer.

Shocking.

"What's next?" she asked. Adrenaline must've worn off because she was starting to feel every ache and the pain was taking the fight out of her. Besides, the chemistry constantly sizzling between them was exhausting.

Holden paced. She waited.

"You make a choice," he finally said. There was so much frustration and warning in his voice.

"I can't go back to Hereford until I know who's trying to kill me," she stated. "I have no idea if this person has access to the main house, but he's made his intentions clear."

"It's best to assume he does, and especially after what happened to your father on the property. I can keep you safe while the sheriff investigates the attempts on your life. Or we can figure out a better way to get you to law enforcement."

She was shaking her head before he finished his sentence.

"If you accept my help that means going off the grid. You have to follow my rules and cut off all communication with everyone but me," he said, and the look in his eyes said he meant every word. "You already know what it's like to be around me. This is what you'll be stuck with until this…*issue* is resolved."

"I'm aware of your magnetic personality," she shot back. She was also aware that he was the only one who seemed capable of keeping her alive. He might not be one to talk much, but it was obvious that he knew how to hide and a piece of her—a piece she should probably ignore—felt safe when he was around.

"Good. Being angry with me will keep us both from making another mistake like the one we made earlier," he said, and his gaze dipped to her lips. He refocused on the patch of wall behind her head.

Did he have to keep reminding her?

"If I can't speak to anyone else, how will the sheriff know what's happened?" she asked.

"I'll arrange for you to give a statement, but it won't be in person," he said. "Then we'll disappear."

She could hire a security company to keep her safe, but there was no time. She needed protection *now*. And it was too risky to give up her location to anyone before she could thoroughly vet the agency's employees. This wasn't the time to chide herself for not thinking of having a security team ready to go sooner. She hadn't needed to consider it before now. Security on the ranch had always proved up to the task until her father...

Thinking about him caused tears to threaten.

Going to the ranch was out. Again, her father had been murdered at home, so someone had slipped past security. Either way, returning to Hereford might not prove good for her longevity.

Her father had trusted Holden Crawford. And that was saying a lot.

"I want your help," she stated. "There are reporters everywhere in Cattle Barge and apparently—" she blew out a frustrated breath "—I'm news. If I surface anywhere, then my face will be all over the internet, on live feeds, and that will lead whoever is after me to my location. I can't afford to be seen right now, and since you seem very good at staying under the radar, you're my best chance at staying alive."

His lips thinned and his gaze narrowed.

"I was afraid you'd say that," he ground out as he walked right past her and out the door.

HOLDEN STALKED OUTSIDE and paced. The room had felt confining, like he was strapped in a straitjacket. Being in the Texas night air always gave him perspective.

Maverick Mike was dead. He'd been killed in a manner that was meant to make a statement. Sure, the man knew how to have a good time. Holden's own father had always gotten a look of appreciation when he'd talked about his poker buddy from Texas. The annual secret game that had happened at Hereford every year was legendary but rarely spoken about. Holden was unclear as to how his father had been included, but he'd been making the trip since Holden could remember. Thinking of Pop brought a wave of anger to the surface. Holden should've been there to stop it. His fists clenched and that familiar sense of frustration bore down on him. Beating himself up over Pop's death again wouldn't change the past.

The door squeaked open behind him. He turned to look at Ella and his heart hammered against his ribs a little harder. The tension of the day was written in the worry lines bracketing her mouth, and Holden had an overwhelming urge to kiss her again. Self-control was normally second nature to him, so his reaction to her threw him off balance.

"Do you think the guys who are after me had anything to do with my father's death?" she asked, and he was grateful for the change in subject.

Was someone planning to systematically kill off the Butler family?

The question was worth considering.

But his noncommittal shrug had the effect of a raging fire in her eyes.

"I'm sorry about throwing my problems in your lap, but why volunteer for this since it's so obvious that it pains you so much to help me?" The spark in her eyes lit something else inside him that he couldn't allow. Holden couldn't go there to that place where he cared about someone again. Not when the two people closest to him were dead because of him.

"There's no need to be sorry," Holden said, unsure of what else he could say in this situation. He'd been away from people for too long and she wasn't making it easy to keep her at arm's length.

The breath she blew out could've put out candles lit across the entire Lone Star State.

Good. Maybe her anger would warn her to keep a safe distance from him.

"You may not realize what it's like for your father to be killed practically under your nose," she said.

Those words lit a fire inside him that no amount of reasoning could extinguish. He stalked toward her until her back was against the wood structure and her lips weren't five inches from his.

"Don't you ever mention my father again," he ground out. "Do you understand me?"

There should be a look of fear on her face because he could damn well be intimidating when he needed to be and he'd released only a tiny portion of what he was capable of. Most people would be shaking right now. Not her. Not Ella. Instead of flinching, her face was soft with compassion. Her arms were at her sides, her hands open.

He planted his palms to either side of her head and practically growled at her.

"I'm sorry for your loss," she said quietly as her cornflower blue eyes rose to meet his. Her honey-wheat hair fell around her shoulders in loose curls. And with that one look, he almost faltered.

Holden, dude, get a grip.

He pushed off the wall and took a couple of steps in the opposite direction. He needed to steer the conversation away from his problems and back to the danger at hand.

"Earlier you said that your father was shot and he was na—" he shifted his gaze back toward her "—not wearing clothes."

"Yes, that's right."

"The sheriff most likely already made the connection that the murderer was making some kind of statement," he said and could see that her mind was clicking.

"Or seeking revenge," she said.

Holden nodded. "I see it like this. Someone wanted the whole world to know that they could access him at his home while he slept." He started pacing again. He could see out of the corner of his eye that she was nodding.

"Did he have a girlfriend?" he asked.

A harrumph noise tore from her throat. "Several, but he seemed to be getting serious with one, Andrea Caldwell."

"Did she know about the others?" he asked.

"Yes," she replied.

"Since a male attacked you, it's probably safe to rule her out," he said.

"Right after my father's murder the sheriff asked for a list of employees, family, friends who might've been there that night. We were putting it together when the room started spinning and my mouth felt dry. I had to get out, to go take a walk," she said. "He was gone by the time I got back."

Holden ignored the fact that he'd felt the same way a few minutes ago. *Almost ignored*, a little voice reminded—a voice he tamped down the second it made itself known. That her stress reaction was similar to his had registered. Fine. The knowledge would help him memorize her habits and reactions, and that could mean the difference between life and death at some point. Holden filed away those facts with others he knew about Ella. She was strong, independent and intelligent.

"Did you ever complete that list and turn it in?" he asked.

"May, our housekeeper, was still working on it with me," she said and then a different kind of emotion lit behind her eyes—concern. "She's probably worried sick after my disappearance and then the news story about my attack. I need to contact her and let her know that I'm okay."

And now Ella was pacing, too.

"Out of the question," he said.

"I wouldn't tell her where I am. Just that I'm safe," she defended.

"We don't take any unnecessary risks. The man who tried to shoot you meant business and I won't—"

Her hand came up as if to stop him and her gaze dramatically swept down across her thigh. "Save your breath. I already know that."

Holden didn't want to look at those long legs of hers.

"She's looked after me since I was a baby. She's like a mother to us. Please figure out a way to get a message to her and let her know that I'm not lying in a ditch somewhere because that's what she's thinking. She's getting older and I can't stand the thought of her worrying herself sick," she said with eyes that pleaded.

And it was working. He thought about Rose, the friend of his father's who Holden had known all his life. He hadn't been in contact with her since he'd been on the run, and now he wondered how many sleepless nights she'd spent worrying about him.

Hell, he was beginning to see how Ella managed to get her way with people. It was a combination of her arguing skills, concern for others and passion. She gave the impression that she cared deeply about others and that was compelling. Those eyes didn't hurt either.

"No." He needed to see that she would listen to him even when she didn't agree. Not even Holden could keep someone alive who was determined to work against him.

She balked and her cheeks reddened with anger, but to her credit she didn't continue to argue her point.

"And don't get any ideas about going behind my back," he said, testing her further. "I'll know."

"How?" she blurted out.

"Trust me. I will," he stated.

Ella stalked past him again, wearing a path in the dirt.

"Fine," she said. "But when are you going to start actually trusting me?"

Chapter Six

Holden had no response. No one had ever been able to read him that well, and especially not someone who barely knew him. Never mind that he felt a deeper connection to Ella Butler than anyone he had ever known. He pushed it out of his mind and chalked it up to them being in similar situations.

Ella's hand came up. "I get it. This is real and you need to feel like you know me. I'm not going to betray you. In case you haven't already figured it out, I need you right now more than you need me. So I won't mess up and risk forcing you to walk away for your own safety's sake. I get what's on the line here for both of us."

Well, those words did a lot toward building a tentative bridge of trust.

"Whatever has you on the run has also caused you to stop believing that you can rely on people," she continued.

He begrudgingly nodded. She was intelligent and observant. He could use that to their advantage.

"Even if it means nothing to you right now, I give you my word that I'll do whatever you ask. Whoever is after me could also be targeting my brothers and sister. They're safely out of the public eye right now, and I'll do whatever it takes to protect them," she said with a defiant sparkle in her eyes.

"Family blood runs thick. I get it," he started.

"Do you really?" she asked. "Because I'm beginning to think that all you know is how to be alone."

He started to tell her that his personal life was none of her business but thought better of it. "What about you? Where is your boyfriend in all this because I need to know if someone else is going to interfere?"

"I don't have one," she admitted. Her cheeks flushed.

Relief washed over him and he chalked it up to the kiss, not wanting to admit how truly interested he'd been in her answer.

A thought struck him. She needed to see that he trusted her with information and he could give up a little. "My mother took off when I was little and I wouldn't know her if she walked past me. I don't have biological brothers or sisters. At least, none that I know of."

He had no plans to elaborate further.

"But I understand and appreciate your loyalty to

yours." His comfort zone had been shattered twenty minutes ago, but she'd been painfully honest with him and he figured he owed her something in return. "And your loyalty to me until this mess is untangled is your best chance at staying alive."

"We're in agreement," she said.

Holden remembered her telling him that she'd been good at campaigning for what was important to her. He could hand it to her. She'd gotten more out of him in the little time he'd known her than any other human had gotten out of him in months. He wasn't much into sharing.

He could also admit to admiring her inner strength as much as he could appreciate that she was a beautiful woman. Okay, where'd that last part come from? *The heart*, that annoying little voice supplied. Time to shut it down and turn it off—whatever *it* was. Holden refused to think that he could have real feelings for her, for anyone, and especially not someone he barely knew. He didn't believe he could be that cruel to another person again. And he needed to get this conversation back on track and off this slippery slope of feelings.

"Earlier, you mentioned the list," he said. "Did any of the names stick out to you?"

"Not really." She blew out a breath and it was like a balloon deflating. "My father was well liked and just as well hated, I guess. Depends on which side of the fence you stand on. If he was your friend, there was no one better. If you crossed him, he would have nothing to do with you. He was dating a few women but he seemed keen on Andrea. I got the feeling that he was getting close to making a real commitment to her."

"Could she have gotten tired of waiting?" he asked.

"I suppose. But she's a good person. And, like you said, she couldn't be the one who attacked me." Her proud shoulders were starting to curl forward and dark circles had formed underneath her eyes. A good look at her said she was exhausted.

"Let's finish talking about this inside," he said and wasn't surprised she didn't put up a fight.

Ella accepted the arm he held out. Her grip was weakening, so he wrapped his arm around her waist to absorb her weight. It was probably a mistake for their bodies to be anywhere near this close to each other. Heat sizzled between them despite the amount of energy it took for her to walk.

"Thank you, by the way. Again. For saving my life," she said quietly.

"Not necessary," he said.

She gave him a look and he quickly added, "It's the least I can do for someone who needs a hand up. Our fathers knew each other and that's how I know yours. When I reached out, he didn't hesitate to help me. I owe him for that."

That seemed to ease her stress and she rewarded

him with a warm smile. He helped her inside and to the bed in the corner. "I have a few supplies on my bike. I'll be right back."

She winced as she scooted her back against the wall in obvious pain.

Holden retrieved his pack from his motorcycle. He had several clean rolled-up T-shirts that he positioned as a pillow for Ella. The bed might be hard but she could at least put her head down on something soft. "This is a far cry from what you're used to on the ranch."

"If you really think that then you have no idea how I spent my childhood," she quipped, and he could see a flash of humor in her eyes. She quickly reeled in her smile but he liked the curve of her lips when she was happy, fleeting as it might've been.

"And how was that, exactly?" He went to work on her leg, cleaning the area with wipes and dabbing the ointment generously. Being prepared for the possibility that he'd have to patch himself up at some point, he was grateful for the medical supplies he kept on hand. He used a patch of white gauze and medical tape to cover the wound.

"In a tent in the backyard," she said. "More bluebonnets than you could count in the spring and we'd come in with more bug bites than should be allowed. But we liked being outside and when we got old enough, Dad would let us build a fire." She shook her head before curling on her side. "May would be so furious with him that she'd sit up half the night in the screened-in porch watching over us. Dad sure didn't make her job easy."

"Sounds like a good way to live if you ask me," he said. But before they could get too far off course and mired in nostalgia he added, "I'm guessing security is lighter around the barn area of the property."

"Dad liked his privacy. He didn't want anyone, and that included his security team, too entangled in his personal affairs," she stated. "He liked to be able to come and go as he pleased without his extra-curricular life part of our dinner conversation."

He could appreciate that a single man wouldn't want his children waking up to a stranger in the house. He also didn't need to say out loud that was a mistake that had cost her father gravely. He could see that she'd made that connection by the look in her eyes. "The person who did this to him wanted to make a statement with his death."

"I know that we ruled out a woman, but could it be? Someone whose heart he broke?" she asked and her voice was almost hopeful.

"Maybe one of the others figured out he was about to cut them loose and decided to show him," he said without conviction.

"He wanted to create office space for me, my sister and twin brothers. He'd been dropping hints to me that he was at least thinking about retiring from the day-to-day operations of the ranch," she said.

"I can't see a man like Maverick Mike retiring from anything," Holden pointed out.

"True. I got the impression he had other plans. Maybe he was thinking of doing something different. Ever since he'd turned sixty-five he'd been acting strange."

"How so? Like midlife-crisis, go-out-and-buy-a-corvette strange?" he asked.

"Not really. My father never really denied himself cars or much of anything else he wanted. It was more like something was stirring. There was a new excitement in his tone that I hadn't heard in a few years." She shrugged. "At the time I thought it had something to do with Andrea. Maybe he was considering his legacy."

"I owe an apology for what I'm about to say, but from what my father said about yours, Maverick Mike didn't seem the type to wax altruistic. Don't get me wrong, he was a good man on many counts." Holden figured she was remembering her father how she might've wanted him to be instead of the man he was, flawed. He'd done the same with his own father, who also happened to be a good man. It was so easy to forget the imperfections of someone who was never coming back.

"I can see why outsiders would feel that way about him," she said. "But Dad had another side to him that even I rarely ever saw."

"A side that makes you think it's possible for a

scorned woman to wiggle her way into his heart and then try to destroy him?" he asked.

"I learned a long time ago not to put people in boxes, Mr. Crawford," she said as she stared right at him.

He could concede that point. He'd seen himself in the mirror at the diner—the person he'd become—and yet she trusted him, his word. Despite what his appearance might've cautioned her. Having seen it for himself, he was shocked at the transformation. A shave didn't sound like the worst thing.

Maybe it was time to clean up.

"Morning will come early," he said after giving her a protein bar and finishing one off himself.

"Good night, Holden," Ella said before rolling onto her other side so her back was to him.

He shouldn't like the sound of his name on her tongue. Hell, he shouldn't be thinking about her tongue at all.

ELLA WOKE THE next morning thinking about what Holden Crawford had said to her last night. There were so many possibilities roaring through her head as she blinked her eyes open to find an empty room. She pushed up onto her elbows to get a better view and panic roared through her when she realized he was gone.

The makeshift pillow he'd placed underneath her head was still there. She forced herself to stand on shaky legs and ignored the pounding at that spot on her forehead between her eyes. A little bit of rest was almost worse than no sleep. She moved to the door to check on his motorcycle. Relief washed over her when she saw it.

Holden Crawford. She liked the sound of his name.

There was a bottle of water on the kitchen counter and something bright yellow positioned next to it. She moved closer to get a good look—a toothbrush. Funny how little things mattered so much when everything was taken away. Being able to wash her face and brush her teeth, things she took for granted literally every day, suddenly felt like gifts from heaven. Ella brushed her teeth in the sink using water from the bottle and used one of the rolled-up shirts that she'd slept on as a wash rag. She doused it and washed her face. The cool liquid felt so good on her skin. Next, she poured water into her hair and then finger-combed it, figuring that was better than nothing.

The door opened and Holden walked in, balancing two tin mugs of what looked like coffee.

"It's strong," he said, holding out the offering.

"Good. I need it," she replied, taking the cup and wasting no time sipping. Seriously, this was heaven in a cup. "How do you do this? It's amazing."

"Let's just say I've had a lot of practice," he said

with a look that seemed so lonely and yet so resigned at the same time.

"Why is it you have two cups?" she asked. "Being that you've been alone for a while."

He chuckled and it was a low rumble from deep in his chest. "I always have a backup for the important things. I never know how quickly I'll have to abandon a place. Plus, one's always clean and ready to go."

"Makes sense," she said after another sip of the fresh brew. "This is the best coffee I've ever had."

He produced another protein bar.

"In your condition, boiled mud would taste good." He laughed a low rumble from his chest and it sent goose bumps racing up her arms.

"I doubt it," she countered, taking the offering and finishing it in a few bites.

"There's something about coffee brewed over an open fire that makes it taste better," he conceded, rewarding her with a smile.

"Not better. Heavenly," she said, returning the friendly gesture. "I've been thinking about everything that's happened to me, my father."

"What did you come up with?" he asked.

"My father's murder seemed planned and, as you already said, like someone wasn't just making sure he was dead. He or she was making their frustration known."

Holden nodded, listening. For someone who, by

his own admission, wasn't great at talking, he excelled at listening.

"My attacks seem just as calculated. And so we have to decide if these two could possibly be linked," she continued. "Maybe he planned my father's murder and now wants to get rid of his heirs, or doesn't feel the need to take extra precautions with me. Maybe this person is just interested in taking me out and possibly my siblings next. We don't know if the others have been targeted and won't until I make contact." She brought her hand up. "Which I won't do unless you say it's okay, and besides, I don't have a phone. But if we figure out who killed my father, then we might be led to the guy who's after me and possibly them. And I'm making myself sick with worry about what might happen next. What if they get hurt or worse because I didn't warn them? How could I live with myself?"

He waited until he seemed sure she was finished.

"I understand if you want to search for the person who killed your father," he said. "The sheriff is already on the case and could have an answer soon."

"I keep going back and forth in my mind, but there must be some link, right?"

He shot her a look that said he wasn't convinced. "I recommend focusing our energy on who's coming after you."

"I guess I'm not much good to my father's investigation if I'm dead," she conceded.

"Won't happen on my watch," he said, and she believed that he meant it. She wished for half of his confidence. "It'll be best if you call in your statement to the sheriff. He might offer to arrange witness protection and you should consider it. After all, you're a high-profile case and you're being targeted. The feds will most likely offer assistance."

"What about you?" she asked, a little stunned at the suggestion.

"I can't go near anyone in law enforcement," he said emphatically. "And I need you to leave it at that."

Ella stopped herself from asking why. "I won't ask for details you're not willing to give. But I'm curious why you think law enforcement wouldn't help you, too."

"Simple. Because the evidence they have makes them believe I'm guilty of something I didn't do." He looked at her dead on.

She did her best not to flinch at his last words. "There's more to the story, though."

"Hell, yeah. But they think they've done their jobs. All I have to contradict the investigation is my word and the knowledge that I'm innocent," he said, and she figured that was more than he'd planned to say by the way he leaned forward and placed his elbows on his knees. That was a move reserved for people who felt exposed.

Ella took a sip of coffee, and it was pretty much a stall tactic so she could think hard about her next words. She didn't want to anger the man who was helping her or offend him. But she'd always been bad at holding her tongue. "You don't strike me as the kind of person who would just check out and give up so easily." He started to say something but she held out her hand, palm up. "Hold on. Before you get upset with me. Hear me out."

He nodded but she could tell there were a whole string of words backing up on the tip of his tongue. Lucky for her, he bit them back.

"You've put yourself in jeopardy twice to save me, and I'm someone you've never met." She made eyes at him. "Granted, you knew my father but he's gone. You didn't have to come back that second time. So as much as you want me to believe otherwise, you're not a bad person."

He opened his mouth to speak but she pointed her index finger at him.

"You're about to mention my father," she stated, already figuring out his next argument based on the look in his eyes.

Holden nodded this time, making a frustrated-looking gesture about being forced to hold his tongue.

"I know what you're thinking and it's not true. You already repaid the debt to him," she said. "You didn't have to come back even if you blamed yourself for dropping me off. You're a decent man no matter how much you blame yourself for whatever happened in the past. I understand why you refuse to go there with a stranger. You say it's because you're afraid for me, but it's so much more than that."

"Oh, yeah?" Holden crossed his massive arms over his chest. "Enlighten me."

"From my point of view, you're afraid to let anyone else in," she stated. She was finished so she steadied herself for his argument, bracing herself against the counter.

Except now, Holden Crawford really was mute.

Chapter Seven

"Since you know me so well, tell me, what's our next step?" Holden asked the woman who left him scratching his head. She was perceptive and thought she'd figured him out. She was wrong. Keeping her at a distance was more for her benefit than his. It was the best way to protect her and keep her safe.

Wasn't it? Or was there a shred of truth to her words?

"We find a way to tell the sheriff what happened last night," she stated, interrupting his thoughts. "In order to do that, we have to leave here. How's that for starters?"

"Obvious but decent," he responded.

"Okay, so where will we go? You've been successfully hiding in rural areas for a while, so I'm guessing you'll stick to what you know. We'll stay somewhere around here." She had a self-satisfied grin and just enough defiance in her eyes to rile him up.

"Sorry. No dice," he stated. "We leave Texas. That's a given. I have a contact in New Mexico who will put us up. I want to stay close and keep my ear to the ground for a few days but we need to stay on the move. We'll head south for an hour and then stop to make the call to the sheriff. Then we can retrace our steps and head west. If the sheriff is going to catch this person, his best chance is while the trail is still hot. If he hasn't made progress in a few days, a week, then we'll have to find a way to get answers ourselves. Interfere too soon and we might hamper his investigation."

"Is this New Mexico person you're referring to a woman by chance?" Ella asked, and there was a mix of emotion playing out behind her eyes that he couldn't quite pinpoint.

"As a matter of fact, yes. Why?" He couldn't wait to hear the answer to this.

She shrugged him off but he could've sworn that she'd bristled. "Curious."

And then it hit him. She was worried they were about to be on their way to see a woman he'd *spent* time with. "She's—"

"None of my business," Ella stated.

"A friend of my father's," he continued. It was important to him that she knew the truth for reasons he didn't want to analyze. "She was sixty-seven on her last birthday."

Ella's cheeks flushed and he forced himself not to

think about how attractive it made her, how attractive she already was.

"Finish your coffee. We need to get on the road," he said, harsher than he'd intended.

An hour south, he stopped off at the first mega-convenience store and bought a cell phone with pre-paid minutes before returning to Ella outside. "Using this will keep us under the radar. If the call is somehow tracked, which should be impossible, we'll take the precaution of tossing it away as soon as we're done. Do you know the numbers of your brothers or sister?"

"Without my cell?" Ella shifted her weight to her left foot and her gaze darted up and to the left. "How sad is it that I tap on a name when I want to call someone and don't remember phone numbers anymore?"

"What about the ranch?" he asked.

"That one I know. It hasn't changed since we had to memorize our phone number and address in elementary school," she stated. "Are you saying I can call home?"

Holden handed over the cell and nodded.

After punching in numbers and listening for someone to pick up, her face lit up.

"May, it's me, Ella." Her excitement was barely contained. The sparkle in her eyes matched.

Holden dropped his gaze to the ground and listened.

"I'm fine, but please don't tell anyone that I called

other than my brothers and sister." She paused for a beat. "I promise that I'm okay. Do I have your word?" Another few seconds passed. "So you have heard from all three of them? And they're okay."

Ella looked at Holden, so he brought his gaze up to meet her gaze. She nodded and smiled. The relief in her expression detailed just how much she loved her siblings.

"The next time you talk to them, tell them to stay out of sight until the sheriff figures this out," she said into the phone. "And tell them I'll do the same." Another beat passed. "No, tell both of my brothers to stay put. I'm nowhere near the ranch and I won't be. I appreciate that they want to stop whoever's doing this but they can help me more if they stay out of the media and away from danger."

Good. She was giving the right direction.

"Tell them it won't matter because I'm not coming back until this is over," she stated, and there was conviction in her voice—conviction that would keep her brothers alive and she seemed to know it. "Just tell them that I love them both and I'm safe. No one can hurt me because they'll never find me."

Holden had every intention of making sure she kept that promise.

"I'm good," she continued, "and, more important, safe." She glanced up at Holden. "I'm in good hands, May. But that's all I can say right now."

May seemed to accept Ella's answers.

"I need to call the sheriff and give a statement now, so I have to go." Her face morphed and gave the saddest look Holden believed he'd ever seen. It caused his chest to clutch.

"I will," Ella promised. After a few more affirmations into the phone and an almost-tearful goodbye, Ella ended the call. She looked away and Holden gave her a little time to gather herself.

Missing a home like Hereford had to be hell. Holden and his father had moved around during his childhood. His father had served in the military and Holden had signed up the day after graduating from high school. There was no place that made him feel like Ella's Hereford.

Ella spun around and took in a breath. "Okay. I'm ready to call the sheriff now."

The conversation was brief. An all-too-familiar anger rumbled in Holden's chest as he listened to the details of Ella being ambushed and then hunted while she bled. He could hear the fear in her voice as she recounted the scene and her vulnerability made him want to put his hands on the man who was trying to kill her. His own past, the horror that his girlfriend, Karen, had endured, filled his chest with rage. The image of the crime scene flashed in his thoughts— an image that had replayed a thousand times in his nightmares for the past two years. Karen splayed across his bed in a pool of blood, her pajamas torn half off her body. The blade of his KA-BAR jammed through her heart.

"Holden," Ella's voice caught him off guard, breaking through his heavy thoughts.

"Yeah?" he responded, even though his clenched jaw had fought against movement. His hands were fisted at his sides and his muscles pulled taut.

She stood there, examining him, and her penetrating gaze threatened to crack through his walls.

"Are you okay?" she asked.

"I will be." He handed her the helmet and threw his leg over the bike. "Ready?"

BY THE TIME they reached Rose's place near the Texas border in Ruidoso, New Mexico, the desert air was cold and Ella shivered. Eight hours on the back of a motorcycle had seemed to take a toll on Ella, but she didn't complain.

He'd stopped off three times for bathroom breaks but had barely spoken to her. Talking about himself had dredged up memories. Remembering his pain was good because being around Ella made him want to forget, to move on. Karen was dead. His father was dead. Holden had been accused of the murders. Those were the only facts that mattered.

"Rose Naples is an artist who specializes in Southwest art," Holden said to Ella as he parked his motorcycle behind her rustic brown log cabin with a green tin roof. "She's lived here most of her life and she and my father went to elementary school together. They stayed in touch but very few people ever knew about her. She leads a quiet life. We'll have food and shelter."

"After eight hours on a bike, all I need is a hot shower and a soft bed," Ella said. She no doubt picked up on the change in him. Good. She needed to stay at arm's length. "I take that back—the bed doesn't even need to be soft."

He started toward the door and she put her hand on his arm. He ignored the fission of heat that was like a lightning bolt to his heart.

"She'll be safe, right?" she asked. "I mean, us being here won't put her in jeopardy, will it?"

"I wouldn't be here if I thought there was the slightest chance," was all he said as he linked their fingers. "It's best if we act like a couple. And to be safe, we can't stay long. A day or two should give us enough time to let the sheriff do his job or come up with a plan."

The word *couple* sat sourly on his lips. He thought about Karen. It had been two long years since she'd been killed, and that same old rage filled his chest when he thought about not being able to bring her killer to justice. Instead, the coward had framed Holden and gotten away with murder. Twice.

Holden picked up the blue cactus pot and located the spare key Rose kept there for him. The sun dipped below the horizon and his stomach reminded him that it had been a while since lunch.

No one should be able to track them to New Mexico. No matter how dire his situation had become, he'd avoided making contact with Rose. She was all he had left.

Best-case scenario, he and Ella could stay a few days. Worst-case, they would get a few hours and then divert to Big Bend National Park to camp out. It was August and he wasn't convinced that Ella would do well under extreme conditions and especially not with her injuries. She needed guaranteed access to clean water to keep the gashes on her head and her leg from becoming infected.

Holden listened at the door for any signs Rose was inside.

The pump action of a bullet being engaged in a shotgun chamber sounded.

"It's me, Rose. It's Holden."

The light flipped on and the door swung open.

Rose dropped the nose of the weapon and flew toward Holden. He caught her in time to give her a bear hug.

"Holden Crawford, you're alive." Shock widened her tearful green eyes. Droplets streamed down her cheeks even though her smile was wide. She was just as thin as he remembered, and her Southwest style of teal poncho, jeans tucked into boots and lots of turquoise jewelry was intact. "I didn't think I'd ever see you again."

"I couldn't risk getting in touch before now." His heart clutched as he noticed the deep worry lines in her face. "But I'm here and I'm okay."

"I'm so sorry about your father." She wiped tears as her gaze shifted from Holden to Ella.

She stepped back and focused on his companion. "I'm sorry. I promise I have better manners than this. I haven't seen this guy in two and a half years and thought I might never again."

"Rose, I'd like you to meet my girlfriend, Ella," he said. The word *girlfriend* sounded a little too right rolling off his tongue. He felt Ella's fingers tense and she radiated a genuine smile.

"I've heard so much about you," Ella said. "And normally I'd hug you but I don't want to offend you by my smell."

"It won't bother me," Rose quipped. "What happened to the two of you?"

"Lost my wallet camping and Ella came out with a pretty bad injury climbing," Holden said by way of excuse. Rose's narrowed gaze said she didn't buy any of it but she smiled anyway. "Can we bunk here for the night until I arrange a transfer of funds and find another place to stay?"

"Do you really have to ask?" Rose set a balled fist on her right hip and pursed her lips. He knew her well enough to know questions were mounting. And he knew her well enough to realize that she wouldn't ask until he gave her the green light.

"Thank you," Ella said, breaking the tension. "Could I trouble you to use your shower?"

"Of course, dear. Follow me," Rose said. She set her shotgun down and motioned for Ella to follow her. "I've got plenty of clean clothes if you need something fresh to borrow."

"I would love that, actually," Ella said.

The two disappeared down the hall and he poured himself a glass of water.

There were so many holes in Holden's plan to pretend he and Ella were in a relationship. He knew nothing about her and vice versa. The plan that he'd been living by to shut Ella out of his personal life was most likely about to backfire. Rose wasn't stupid and he wanted to tell her more. But Ella's secrets weren't his to share.

Rose returned a couple of minutes later and took a seat at the table in her eat-in kitchen.

Holden followed suit, taking the chair across from her at the round table.

"Where have you been?" She took his hand and squeezed.

"All over," he said.

"I know you didn't do it." She gave him a sincere look. "I've been following the story and there's no way you would've done that to Karen. I know you better than that and started to come forward, but before I could get on a plane I read about what they did to your father."

"I'm glad you stayed put and I appreciate your confidence in me." Gratitude filled Holden's chest.

"Sorry I couldn't attend your father's funeral," she said, twisting her hands. "I was sick about it but he wouldn't have wanted me to go and especially not after the way he was…"

She stopped as though she couldn't say the words.

"No, he wouldn't," Holden agreed. "For the record, that makes both of us."

"You couldn't be there either, could you?" She shook her head and her voice was filled with sadness. Like a heavy rain cloud before the first drop of rain spilled, he decided.

"Not because I didn't want to be," he said.

"Your father got a message to me after Karen was murdered. He said that I should tell you 1-9-6-4. I have no idea what it means. Do you? He also mentioned a place you used to fish but I can't remember where. Now it feels so important but at the time I had no idea."

He shook his head. The numbers didn't register as important or click any puzzle pieces together. "I'll have to think about it. Could be a year?"

"I thought about that, too. But why a year?" One of her brows spiked.

Rose picked up the saltshaker and rolled it in between her flat palms. Then Rose set it down and looked him straight in the eye. "Do you have any inkling why they were killed?"

"Other than to cover for someone who wanted Karen dead and set me up for murder? No," he admitted.

"He must've worried they'd come after him or he wouldn't have sent the message." She focused on the saltshaker. "Guess he thought he could handle them when they did."

"They got to him before I could," he said and then stood.

"Don't go," she said, and she must've realized how difficult it was for him to speak about the past.

He reclaimed his seat. Those same frustrations of getting nowhere with his own investigation enveloped him.

"Who's the girl?"

"My girlfriend." Could he share a little without endangering her?

"How'd the two of you meet?" Her gaze penetrated him.

"I didn't underestimate you, Rose. And you know I'd tell you anything that I could." The thought of defining his relationship with Ella or his need to help her spiked his blood pressure. "I was wrong to come here. We'll leave after she finishes in the shower."

"Maybe it was a mistake to come here because I can read you so well," she said. "I'm not concerned that you hurt Karen. I know that for the lie it is. But

I know you, Holden, and there's something going on between you and Ella. You're not telling me every—"

"You're reading too much into it. She's a friend in trouble. Can we leave it at that?" Trying to continue the charade was going nowhere. Rose knew him too well. His father had brought him to New Mexico every summer. Sometimes they'd stay with Rose. Others they'd camp the entire time. But they always met her for a meal. The woman had watched Holden grow from a young child. It was Rose who had stepped in from afar when his own mother took off. He'd considered Rose a mother figure, if not his mother. And since she knew him so well, he needed to tread carefully when it came to Ella.

"All I'm saying is that I hope you can find a way to forgive yourself for the past—"

He started to argue but she waved him off.

"Two years wandering. Lost. Karen didn't deserve what happened to her, but neither did you. You didn't do anything wrong," she said, and an odd wave of relief washed over him. Strange that one person's opinion mattered so much to him. But it was Rose, and their relationship went way back.

"That means a lot coming from you," Holden said quietly. Was she right? Was he punishing himself by cutting himself off from the world?

"Promise me you'll try to forgive yourself, Holden," she continued.

"When I find the killer and bring him to justice."

She started to protest but he held up a hand.

"As far as she goes, can we leave it alone for now?" He nodded toward the hallway. "Keep up the charade for her sake?"

"My lips are sealed." She pretended to close a zipper over her mouth. "If and when you can talk about it without violating her trust, I'm here for you."

Holden thanked her again, drained his glass and poured another. "Any chance you have an extra razor in that guest bathroom of yours?"

A CLEAN BODY and fresh clothes borrowed from Rose did wonders for Ella's attitude. Holden had disappeared into the bathroom after redressing the bandages on her thigh and forehead. Rose was cooking up something that smelled amazing. Ella's stomach growled so loudly that her cheeks flushed with embarrassment. "Excuse me."

Rose turned and chuckled. She moved to the fridge and pulled out a container of what looked like homemade salsa. After, she poured tortilla chips into a bowl and set both down on the table in front of Ella. "This should help until the food's ready."

Ella immediately dug into the offering. It was good. So good. And nice to be in a safe place. "This is amazing. Thank you."

"I grow the cilantro fresh in pots out back," Rose said, looking pleased. "Makes all the difference in the world."

The older woman moved with grace, and her half dozen bracelets jangled in time with her fluid movements. Her all-white hair was pulled back in a neat ponytail. Turquoise earrings dangled from her ears. She embodied Southwest elegance at its best.

Ella was grateful that Rose seemed content to be together in the same room without the need for conversation. So much had gone on in the past few days that Ella could scarcely wrap her thoughts around it, and she was still trying to break through the fog. She dipped another chip in the homemade salsa, took a bite and savored the taste of the fresh tomatoes.

"Did you grow these, too?"

Rose nodded and smiled.

Ella thought about May. She grew her own garden and said the same things with a similar look of pride. Ella's heart squeezed. She felt naked without her cell phone and she missed home more than she wanted to show. And so many questions loomed, keeping her away from everything she loved.

Why would someone come after her? So far, the others in her family were safe. Ed Staples, the family's lawyer, had promised May that he would help keep the ranch running while Ella was away. Ella had learned that during her phone call with May. He was a good man and close confidant to her father. She could trust him to hold up his end.

"I'll get you started eating." Rose interrupted Ella's

thoughts. The older woman set a plate down in front of Ella and then motioned toward the chili peppers. "I wasn't sure which you liked, red or green, so there's both."

"That's perfect," Ella said, accepting the literally mouthwatering chalupa. She dug in immediately and the shredded chicken was tender beyond belief. The covering of homemade guacamole was smooth and creamy in her mouth. And she already knew the salsa on top was in a whole new class of Tex-Mex.

"It's Holden's favorite dish, chalupas." Rose went back to work, humming while she deep-fried what had to be his.

"He talks about your guacamole all the time," Ella offered, pretending she knew more about her "boy-friend" than she actually did.

"Really? He's been allergic to avocados since he was seven years old." Rose didn't turn around but her humming picked up.

Ella figured trying to save herself after that slip was futile, so she focused on her food. Her back was to the hallway, so she didn't see Holden when he first entered the room. She had a big bite in her mouth when she turned around and it took everything inside her not to spit it out. She covered her mouth as she finished chewing and swallowed. "Holden?"

He seemed almost embarrassed by her reaction.

"Sorry," she quickly added. "It's just… I've never seen…you look…" She could feel herself digging a hole as the right way to frame this conversation didn't hit her. What did strike her was how drop-dead gorgeous Holden Crawford was underneath all that untamed facial hair. She'd seen a hint of it before in his eyes—those bold blue irises. "Your face. You look…good."

"I thought you should finally see what you're getting yourself into," he said easily, and she realized that he was covering for her slip, her second mistake. There was a slight curve to his lips, not exactly a smile but a hint of one. He walked right over to her and kissed her on the forehead. The second his soft lips touched her skin, a thunderclap of need rocketed through her.

All she could do was look up at him, mute, with a dry throat. It suddenly felt like she'd licked a glue stick.

Holden had that strong square jaw that most women obsessed over, and she could admit that it looked damn good on him. She already knew he had a body made for athletics. He had stacked muscles that surfers, or anyone who wore very little clothing for their sport, would lust after. She had to force her gaze away from his lips. *Okay, come on.* This was getting a little ridiculous. It wasn't like Holden was the first attractive man Ella had ever seen. Of course, she'd never met one with his sex appeal and magnetism before. And she'd spent a few days with him already so she needed to pick her jaw up off the floor and get a grip.

Out of her peripheral she could see that Rose continued on with her work, ignoring the show of affection on display for her benefit, and for a split second she wondered if the woman was on to them.

Holden took a seat next to Ella, his right thigh touching hers, and the contact sent warmth to all kinds of places that didn't need to be aroused at the dinner table of such a kind stranger.

Ella needed to redirect her energy. She studied her chalupa as she dug into another bite.

"Do you grow your own chili peppers?" she asked Rose, and her voice came out a little strained.

"Is there any other way?" Rose quipped with a satisfied smirk.

"Your food is the best thing I've ever tasted aside from Holden's coffee," she said.

"Thank you." Rose had cleaned up the last of the dishes. "It's late, so I'll make up the guest room for you two."

Rose padded down the hall.

Right. Ella and Holden were supposed to be a couple and couples slept together. With his leg touching hers and the way he'd just looked at her, she almost believed the lie herself.

Ella finished up the food on her plate, surprised that she could eat a bite let alone empty the plate so quickly. "So, you're allergic to avocados?"

"No." He seemed confused at first but then he cracked another smile. "That what Rose told you?"

She nodded.

He shook his head. "She's a tricky one."

"A little too smart for her own good if you ask me," Ella said, feeling the burn in her cheeks. Or was that a simple reaction to the attractive man sitting next to her.

It didn't take long for Holden to finish the food on his plate, guacamole and all.

Rose reappeared in the hallway. "Leave the dishes. I'll take care of those."

Ella started to protest but Rose shut her down.

"Found a couple of unused toothbrushes in my cupboard. Leftovers from visits to the dentist over the years. I used to save them to use on trips but I haven't wanted to leave home in more years than I want to admit," the older woman continued.

"I can see why. You have a beautiful home," Ella said with true appreciation. The style of this place reflected that of its owner—elegant Southwest.

Holden stood, rinsed off their plates and linked his hand with Ella's as he led her down the hallway after Rose. She tried, rather unsuccessfully, to ignore the chemistry fizzing between them.

"I put fresh sheets on the bed, so you should be good," Rose said, stepping aside so they could enter the bedroom.

Ella wasn't sure what she'd been expecting to find. It was a bedroom after all.

But seeing one bed with turned-down sheets sent her pulse thundering.

Chapter Eight

"I can take the couch," Holden offered as soon as Rose disappeared down the hallway, figuring him and Ella alone in a bed might not be the best way to get a night of rest.

Ella stared at the bed for a thoughtful minute and then stepped inside the room. "It'll be best if we both get a good night's sleep and someone your size won't fit on the sofa. Plus, Rose will get the wrong idea about us being in a relationship. No reason to raise suspicion because that would be bad for her in the long run."

"I could always tell her we had a fight," he said, his gaze stopping on the base of Ella's throat where he could see her pulse pounding. And that wasn't helping matters for him one bit.

"It's okay," she said. "I trust you."

He hoped she wasn't making a mistake because he could tell she meant those words even though she'd said them so low he practically had to strain to hear.

She climbed into bed and turned onto her side, facing the opposite wall. She smelled like flowers and citrus, clean and like spring. Holden was already in trouble because he liked Ella Butler, and any kind of a relationship, no matter how short-lived it would be, was a slippery slope best avoided.

He pushed the covers aside and moved to the spot next to her. She rolled over and curled her body around his left side. Flat on his back, she nestled into the crook of his arm and rested her head on his chest.

Freezing up when a woman shared a bed with him was foreign to Holden, but then he'd never been in this circumstance before. In the past, a warm body beside him, hell, curled around him, meant two consenting adults who equally wanted to be there. Expectations were clear on both sides: great sex. This was not the same. The water was muddy with Ella. She wanted to be home, not there with him, but had to stay away in order to live.

Holden could hear her breathing and almost convinced himself that she was asleep until her eyes slowly opened and she looked up at him. That's all it took for him to do what he knew he shouldn't. He dipped his head down and claimed her mouth. Her lips parted and he delved his tongue inside, tasting her sweet honey. Her tongue teased him and she sucked on his bottom lip before gently biting. Need stirred from deep within. He wrapped his arms around her and hauled her tight against his chest. Her body fitted his, melding against him perfectly, and he could hear her breathing quicken.

Her hands were on his chest, her fingertips sliding along the ridges of muscles there. It would be so easy to let go with her...

Karen popped into his thoughts. Her lifeless body lying in the bed they'd shared the night before, and his eyes shot open as he pushed up to his elbows. Ella was still partially tangled up with him so she repositioned, curling her legs around his midsection and balancing by digging her hands into his shoulders rather than spill off his lap.

"Not a good idea" was all he could manage to say.

Face-to-face, her minty toothpaste washed over him with every quick breath. She had that all-too-familiar hungry look in her eyes.

"Really, Holden?" she asked.

"This is getting out of hand," he said through ragged breaths. His body argued that a night of hot sex with Ella—and he was pretty damn certain it would rock his world—would be all he needed to get past his attraction to her and move on so he could focus on what was important: saving her life. And he could almost convince himself that once the mystery was gone, it would somehow become easier to be around her without so much sexual chemistry firing between them, distracting him. But that logic was as smart as pouring gasoline onto a forest fire and expecting to curb the flames. Laws of physics dictated a raging inferno.

"I'm confused," Ella said, and he could see the emotion in her eyes—eyes that were so expressive she was easy to read.

For lack of a real answer, he said, "So am I."

She crawled off his lap and curled onto her side again, hugging the edge of the bed. He mumbled another apology but she didn't respond. He repositioned onto his back and stared at the ceiling. He might be the dumbest man alive because not having sex with Ella wasn't exactly stopping him from thinking about the soft curve of her hips when they'd pressed against him. Nor did the intensity of their chemistry ease. Being with her was like sleeping with fireworks under the blanket.

Holden sighed harshly. If only he hadn't gone jogging at five that morning twenty-five months ago. Karen would be alive and so would his father.

By the time sunlight peeked through the blinds, he heard Rose padding down the hall toward the kitchen. Ella was still asleep based on her even breathing and he didn't want to wake her, so he peeled off the covers and slipped out of bed.

Rose was in the kitchen with a fresh pot of coffee brewing that he smelled from the bathroom where he stood at the sink brushing his teeth. His thoughts had bounced around last night. Most of them entailed how sweet Ella's silky skin felt against his body. The silhouette of her sweet round bottom had broken his concentration more than once. He dozed off in fits and starts because something was trying to break through. Something was bugging him. And he couldn't pinpoint what that something was. It was frustrating the hell out of him. He'd lost perspective and he needed to talk about it. He hoped a strong cup of coffee could clear his head.

"Morning," he said to Rose as he walked into the kitchen.

She nodded and caught his eye. "I haven't seen you this twisted up since you were in the eighth grade and that girl—what was her name? Tara—went off with your friend because she was convinced you didn't like her. And you did like her. But once you realized your friend did, too, you knew that you could never ask her out."

If only his problems could be that simple again, deciding between a hot girl and loyalty to his best friend. Holden had made the obvious choice—loyalty. But it had felt like a huge sacrifice at the time.

"I was awake chewing on something all night," he said. He could talk the basics of the case through without giving exact details or violating Ella's trust. "In a murder case, investigators always look to the people closest to the victim, to their inner circle, and work outward from there."

"True," she said, and she would know because her father had spent his entire life working for the Santa

Fe Police Department. "Tell me more about this person's family. What are they like?"

"I couldn't say, personally. They seem to care for each other on the surface. There are twin brothers and a younger sister in this situation." He appreciated Rose going along with him without asking if they were talking about Ella.

"Does this have anything to do with what you're going through?" Rose studied him before taking a sip of coffee.

"No. This is different," he clarified. "There's no tie. This person's siblings seem to care. Both of her brothers had wanted to drop what they were doing and come to her but she'd convinced them that it would be too risky. They might lead the men targeting her right to her. Her sister shared a similar sentiment."

"So, let's rule out the immediate family," she said. "You've no doubt considered who stands to gain from her death."

"That's where things get complicated. Her father is wealthy. He was recently murdered and an attempt was made on her life almost immediately after," he said.

"She was the only one targeted out of four children?" A gray eyebrow hiked.

"The others left as soon as news of their father's death broke. She stayed to run the ranch," he supplied, holding back the fact that her father hadn't been gone for a whole week when she'd been attacked.

"All the siblings are out of town and that's not a convenient excuse?" she asked.

"I don't believe so."

"And that's where everything gets confusing, isn't it?" She picked up the spoon on the table and stirred her coffee absently. Rose always did that when she didn't have a good answer. There was so much comfort in knowing someone well enough to know their little quirks.

Holden had been away from civilization far too long. On balance, he had to consider if he was really living at all or just existing. Hiding. He raked a hand over his shaved chin, half expecting his beard to still be there and feeling nothing but exposed skin.

"Let's circle back then, to the actual attempt on the victim," Rose said. "What were the circumstances?"

"A rock was thrown at her head and she was left to die while hiking alone," he supplied.

Rose's eyes lit up. "That tells me whoever did this wanted to make it look like an accident, so they have something to lose. It could be more than just status in the community."

"I thought that, too, until she was shot at on the way to the sheriff's office to give a statement a couple of days later," he said.

"Killer might've been expecting that. He goes

back for the body where she was hiking. Doesn't find one, so he camps around the sheriff's office, figuring she might've gotten a good enough look at him to give a description," she said. "She shows and he figures he has to take her out. He's afraid to leave a possible witness."

"Good points." Holden reached for his beard again. Halfway there he realized he'd shaved and stopped as he held out his hand awkwardly in midair. "I suspect you're right and this person wants to keep his place in the community."

ELLA STRETCHED SORE muscles and pain rifled through her thigh. Her hand shot to the spot as she grimaced and blew out a breath. Contact was a bad idea even though all she touched was gauze and tape.

There'd most likely be some pain relievers in the kitchen and, more important, caffeine. More movement was going to hurt. *Time to suck it up, buttercup.*

Forcing herself to move her legs against all the resistance her body was giving seemed like the worst of bad ideas. Movement took every bit of effort inside her. Ella cursed under her breath and repeated the word a few more times as she pushed off the bed. Brushing her teeth was the first respite she had from the stabbing pain as she leaned her weight against the counter. Even her hip was sore. And all that screaming pain distracted her from the monster-sized headache raging between her temples.

After turning off the water, she heard the low hum of Holden's voice coming from the kitchen, and awareness trilled through her and her cheeks burned with embarrassment. She'd practically thrown herself at him last night and he'd stopped abruptly. She'd blame the entire episode on herself except that she'd seen that momentary flash of terror in his eyes that he tucked so masterfully behind that steel-jawed facade before rejecting her. She'd be angry with him for the rejection—and part of her was—but he'd said the last person he'd cared about ended up dead because of him, and she sensed that he couldn't go there with her and especially not under the circumstances.

He was right, though. Her life was complicated enough right now without adding to the confusion with a romantic entanglement with the man keeping her alive. Emotions were heightened. She needed to focus on being grateful to him and nothing more.

That's as far as she planned to allow her feelings for Holden Crawford to go.

Hopefully she'd be able to stick to her plan.

Chapter Nine

"We're leaving today. We'll pack up after breakfast," Holden said to Ella as she entered the kitchen. He barely glanced up.

"What's the rush?" Rose stood and moved toward the counter with the coffee maker. She looked to Ella when she said, "Have a seat. I'll get a cup for you."

Ella thanked her and sat next to Holden. The sexual chemistry between them zinged as intensely as ever and her stomach gave a little flip when her knee touched his thigh.

She must've also winced with movement when she sat because Holden stopped what he was doing and said, "You're in pain."

"A little," she admitted.

"I have something for that. I'll make something to eat first," Rose said, handing over a fresh mug. "Doc is always warning me about taking ibuprofen on an empty stomach."

"Thank you." Ella stared into the brown liquid

before taking a sip. Anything to take the focus off how she felt whenever Holden was near and the assortment of aches and pains her body had racked up. She took a sip, enjoying the burn. "This is so good."

The breakfast burritos were equally wonderful.

"I have a few errands to run in town this morning," Rose said. "Can I pick up anything for you?"

Holden's gaze flicked up and held. "Do me a favor?"

She nodded. "Anything."

"Don't mention having houseguests." The concerned look on his face seemed to resonate with the older woman.

"Not a problem," she said before grabbing her keys off the counter and her purse off a hook positioned near the back door. "I'll only be a couple of hours. Will you be here when I return?"

"Yes," he said.

Relief washed over Ella as the older woman smiled and disappeared through the door. No way would she want to put Rose in danger but she had hoped they could stick around a few days. Being near her, in her calm presence, was comforting. Since Holden had already said they were leaving today, she sipped her coffee and tried not to think about having to get on the back of the motorcycle again.

"She'll be safe, right?" she asked Holden as he studied a laptop screen.

"As long as no one figures out we've been here,

she will be," he said. "And I have every intention of ensuring that she is."

Shock reverberated through Ella as reality once again bore down on her. They were both on the run from dangerous men.

"Where do we go next?" she asked.

"That depends on how your leg's doing and how close the sheriff is to figuring this out." He didn't look up and she took it as a sign that he didn't want to talk.

The physical presence of him was difficult to ignore. He was big and imposing. *And sexy*, a little voice decided to add. It was an annoying little voice, like a fly at a picnic, buzzing around her face. She squashed that bug immediately. Holden Crawford was complicated. Danger practically radiated from his muscled biceps.

She drained her mug and pushed to standing, wincing as she tried to regain her balance, not yet steady on her feet.

"Don't do that," he said, rising to catch her. She had no intention of falling, pain or not.

"My leg is just sore. I need to walk it off," she defended, motioning toward her thigh.

"Mind if I take a look?" His gaze was on her now. The intensity of those honest blue eyes released a thousand butterflies in her stomach. Her throat felt like she'd downed a bottle of glue and her upper lip stuck to her top row of teeth when she managed a weak attempt at a smile. "Okay."

Ella took a seat again and showed him the injury.

Holden set up a few supplies, wipes and antibiotic ointment on the table next to her. She could've sworn he took in a sharp breath and muttered something that sounded like a swear word before he dropped to his knees in front of her.

She flexed her fingers when she thought about how deep the ridges in his shoulders were and how thick that dark hair of his was. Focusing her attention on the investigation would hopefully diffuse some of the sexual tension pinging thickly between them.

"We can't rule anyone out other than my siblings until we hear my father's will," she said.

"I have to consider everyone." His gaze was focused on the tape as he made a move to tear at one of the corners.

"So, what? The entire town is suspect? We'll never figure out who's responsible at this rate. We haven't ruled anyone out in your opinion, and I have no chance of going home anytime soon." She was frustrated and taking it out on him. In part because she needed to keep herself from thinking about doing other things to him. She clasped her hands and forced them on her lap. Thoughts of missing her father, of missing her family and of missing home struck a hole in her chest.

Holden tugged at the medical tape. A patch of

skin pulled up along the tear line. As light as the touch might've been, she could've been hit by a bolt of lightning for the effect it had on her skin. A trail scorched from contact and her entire thigh warmed and zinged with awareness. Other places did, too, but she was determined not to think about those.

"Does this hurt?" His gaze flicked up to hers.

"That? No." There was so much going on inside her emotionally that the pain in her leg barely registered. She was having a difficult enough time fighting the barrage of tears threatening. Her thoughts were a jumbled mess spanning everything from his rejection to how much she wished life could go back to the way it was two weeks ago.

"Not the whole town, just people who would benefit from you disappearing." Holden went back to work.

"Like the people who work for us?" she asked.

"If they fit the bill. I was thinking more along the lines of projects you're involved in that impact other people." He dabbed antibiotic ointment along the gash, which looked like a crack in her skin.

"Ranch business impacts a lot of people, provides a lot of jobs directly and indirectly," she said.

"Any vendors who've been cut out of the pie recently?" He took scissors to a gauze pad, cutting it down to fit her wound.

"No. We've been doing business with most of our suppliers for years. Many are second- or third-generation owners." Thinking hurt. "We pay all our bills on time."

Ella must've made a face because he froze.

"Did that hurt?" He lifted the bandage slowly.

"No."

"I know you're upset and that's partly my fault. I let things get too far last night and I regret it," he started.

"Don't give me a speech about how there's nothing wrong with me. That you're just not attracted to my type," she quipped with more anger than she'd intended. "I'm sure you haven't been with a woman in a long time since you've been on the run."

His gaze locked onto hers.

"For your information, there've been plenty of women since I've been off the grid, just none that I could really care about. That doesn't happen often for me," he said, the intensity of his gaze washing over her like a rogue wave.

"Really? Maybe it's your magnetic personality," she bit out sarcastically, still fuming.

"Probably." He leaned back on his heels and placed his hands on his massive thighs, elbows out. "But the last person I cared about was killed by the men tracking me and I'm no closer to figuring out why now than I was two years ago. My father was also killed before I could get to him, which you already know but those thoughts keep rewinding inside my head."

His words sucked the wind out of her and all she could manage to say was, "Oh."

"So, yeah, I don't want to care about you and I'm frustrated because you're smart and beautiful with a body made for sinning on Sundays but none of that matters." His gaze was searing her skin as his eyes traveled her body. "Because if I allow myself to get soft enough to actually care what happens to you beyond blind loyalty to your father, you might end up dead, too. And I can't do that to another person. Not again. I wouldn't survive. There's enough blood on my hands."

"In case you haven't noticed, I don't need to worry about *your* men chasing after me. I seem to have attracted my own jerk intent on doing me harm all by my lonesome," Ella barked, ignoring the shivers racing up her arms with Holden this close. "I'm guessing someone wants to see my family suffer or has something to gain by targeting me after killing my father, but I have no idea what or who. So how's that for infuriating?"

"You should probably calm down," Holden said.

And that was like pouring gasoline on a fire. Ella pushed to her feet quickly.

"Because what? I'll raise my blood pressure? Have a heart attack?" She was really getting worked up now, like an out-of-control wildfire she couldn't douse, the flames roaring inside her. "In case you haven't noticed, I may not live to see tomorrow so I'll scream all I want."

Holden pushed up to his feet, too, and was standing inches away from her. She could see his chest rise and fall rapidly as his hands came up to cup her face.

"Because we'll make mistakes if we let emotions override rational thinking. It's best for Rose if no one knows we're here. I'm thinking about doing what's right for her, for you." There was something so calming about his physical presence. "Not kissing you is taking what little self-discipline I have left after last night, but I'm not doing it *because* I care about you. We'll figure out who's after you and I'll make sure the person responsible is locked away for a very long time or buried ten feet under. It'll be his choice. But, damn it, when this is over, I have every intention of walking away from you and never looking back."

His gaze had narrowed and his lips thinned.

Ella grabbed a fistful of his T-shirt, her knuckles meeting a wall of muscle.

"You may be able to stop yourself from kissing me but what will you do, Holden Crawford, when I kiss you?" she asked, locking onto his gaze. Her cheeks flushed against his hungry stare. And she might be baiting a bull, but she didn't care.

"It would be a mistake on your part," he said. His eyes had that dark, hungry look she'd seen moments before the first time he'd kissed her.

"What makes you say that?" she continued, knowing full well that she was enticing him.

"Because you don't have any idea what you're really asking for," he stated. And then he turned away from her and sat down at the laptop.

Neither frustration nor rejection would stop Ella at this point. She took the couple of steps toward Holden and straddled his thighs. He could ignore her once they were face-to-face.

"I'm a grown woman. You're a consenting adult male," she said, and she could see that he was considering her words.

He brought his hands up to grip her hips and her stomach quivered.

"Believe me, you don't want anything to do with me," he said before leaning forward to rest his forehead on hers. "It would be a mistake to think otherwise."

There was that word again. *Mistake.*

He seemed determined to avoid anything good that could happen between them. He couldn't let go of the past and she couldn't compete with a ghost. No amount of logic could change a man who was so strong willed.

Ella stood up.

"Mistakes don't define a person. Everybody makes those. It's part of how we learn. But choices do," she said before walking out of the room.

He could take it or leave it. Ella was done.

AN HOUR HAD passed and Holden still hadn't found the right words to say to Ella about whatever was happening between them. He felt it, too. The current running between them was strong and powerful. And just like a power cord in water, dangerous.

"Why do you really owe my father?" Ella asked as she entered the room.

The question caught Holden off guard.

"I already told you." He didn't look up, didn't need to. She was watching him and he could feel her glare roaming over him. Yeah, she was giving him the signal that would normally make him react differently, but he didn't go into anything deeper than a one-night fling without both parties being completely aware of what they were getting into. Ella Butler was in over her head and had no idea.

He hammered the keyboard.

"No, you didn't. All you said was that you owed him a favor. Why?" she pressed.

"Maybe you weren't listening before in the cabin," he started, but she cut him off with a strangled noise.

"Don't say he put a roof over your head so you wanted to return the favor," she said.

"I wasn't going to. He did a helluva lot more. He could've turned me in with one quick call to law enforcement. He didn't. He knew what he was getting into and he had every right to turn his back. He didn't. Helping me put him directly in danger. I don't know the man from Adam, personally. He and my father were friends. Maverick Mike said he owed my father one and I didn't ask a lot of questions, considering how short on options I was," he said, studying a section of map on the screen, searching for a safe place to camp for a day or two. Exhaustion poured over him and he—once again—fought against it. If he had his druthers, he'd still be at the cabin on the Butler property, the place that had felt like his first real home in longer than Holden could remember. Virginia had never really been the place where he saw himself setting down roots. Although Holden had lived there going on five years before his world had come crumbling down around him. And Karen? He still couldn't believe she was gone. It had all happened so fast.

"Do you ever directly answer a question?" she asked, and he could almost feel the heat oozing off her.

"Yes."

The silence in the room stretched on for longer than he should've allowed. He shook his head and went back to work, scouting locations from the map on the screen. Not any closer to finding an appropriate place to go than he had been an hour ago.

Ella's earlier words kept winding through his thoughts. Was he afraid to let anyone in? No matter how much he wanted to continue to refute them, he couldn't ignore the shred of truth. And he was getting tired of the war raging in his head trying to keep her away.

"I OWE YOU an apology. I'm going stir-crazy sitting around here. My mind is starting to think about all the things I need to do but I can't." Ella paced in the charming kitchen, wringing her hands together. Her chest squeezed thinking about how distant she felt from everything she'd ever known, everything familiar. Work was no doubt piling up. "I feel so disconnected. Normally, my cell is an extension of my hand and I'm feeling panicked without it. My inbox is probably exploding. I guess there's no chance I can check email on that thing." She motioned toward the laptop.

"Your location can be traced back here based on the unique IP address if you access anything personal." Holden shook his head, twisting his lips in an apologetic look. "Nothing matters more to me than keeping you alive, finding out why you're being targeted and ensuring Rose's safety."

"I know we've discussed this before, but have you ruled out my father's killer trying to erase the family?" she asked.

"That's one possibility," he responded. "I'd like to explore a few others. Is anyone upset with you? Have you had any fallings-out with a friend?"

"None that I can think of," she stated. "But honestly, the days leading up to me going hiking are still a blur. I'd just found out about my father and this—" she motioned toward the covered gash on her forehead "—can't be helping."

"Was anyone jealous of you?" he asked.

"People like me overall, I think." She really thought about what he was saying. Could she have upset someone enough for a person to want her dead? The notion that someone she knew could be hunting her sent an icy chill down her spine. "I do a lot of work to give back to the community. I don't always agree with people's opinions and, sure, there are conflicts from time to time within pretty much all my charity work. Anytime you get ten or fifteen different people in the room there are going to be that many opposing views. We argue, debate and then eventually come to a resolution. Does everyone walk away happy? No. But what could possibly warrant this?" She heard her own voice rise defensively.

"It would be easier to pin down the responsible party if we could trace them to you instead of your father," he said.

"I don't know." Flustered, she paced.

"I'm not trying to upset you." He tried to reassure her.

"I know. And what you're saying makes sense," she said, wishing she could will her pounding pulse to calm down.

"What about your friends?" he asked.

"I have a few people who are close but between helping run the ranch and my work with organizations, I don't have a lot of time for happy hour." Hearing her life put in those terms sounded like a sad existence. She felt the need to add, "I spend most of my time with my family."

"You already said that you aren't seeing anyone special." His gaze intensified on the screen. "Are you dating around?"

"I can't see why that would be—"

"Before you get distraught with me I'm only asking to see if there could be a jealous guy in the mix," he added, and he still didn't look at her. "Someone who looks like you would attract a lot of interested men."

"I date a little." She shrugged. The compliment caused her cheeks to heat. "I love living on the ranch and Cattle Barge is home, but there aren't a lot of interesting men around. I grew up there and it's a small town so I dated around in high school and haven't looked back since college. Not a lot of new people move to town unless you count the men who work in the stable, and I would never date inside the ranch. It's bad business and someone would lose their job if things got awkward after."

The only truly good-looking person she'd seen in the past year was a new guy who'd moved to the outskirts of town and kept to himself. But she didn't mention him to Holden.

"And besides, I'm too busy with work and my charities to get out much," she defended. "I haven't been serious about anyone for a long time, and I've been thinking that I need to spend more time in Austin or San Antonio so I can meet someone."

Holden waited for her to finish. She was oversharing. Being nervous had her talking more than she should.

"I'm sure my life sounds awful to someone like you but—"

"Tell me more about your charity work." He leaned back in his chair and finally took his eyes off the screen.

One look from him caused her heart to flutter and she hadn't experienced that with anyone in too long.

"I pick projects that I'm passionate about, especially ones that need a helping hand," she responded, thankful for the redirection.

"What kind?" He folded his arms over a broad chest, and it was the most relaxed she'd seen him since they met.

"Mostly local stuff. Animal rights, various park cleanup and preservation initiatives, our local food bank and charities that serve the elderly in our community," she said.

"Sounds like a lot." His brows shot up.

"Does it?" She shrugged. "I don't know. I see something that needs to be done and I pitch in to help it along."

"The Butler name opens a lot of doors," he said, and she picked up on a hint of sarcasm.

"Yes, it does. If you expect me to be ashamed of

it, you need to think again." Her shaky voice belied the confidence she was trying to project.

"I didn't mean anything by it. I'm sure it helps to have that name behind you," he said.

"It does. And I was born with a silver spoon in my mouth. There. Are you happy?" She went ahead and said it for him…for everyone who'd discounted her because her father had made a show out of giving her everything. Had it been too much? Yes. "If you think wearing nice clothes and being given lavish gifts makes you feel good about yourself or loved, you're wrong. A little girl needs to be held when she cries. Not handed an expensive doll and left alone in her room to sort through her emotions."

"So you're saying that giving a little girl everything she could possibly desire is a bad thing?" Holden asked. "Because if I had a daughter, I'd move heaven and earth to give her the world."

Her stomach gave a little flip at the thought of a newborn wrapped in a pink blanket in the burly man's arms. A thought struck her like a rogue wave…*their daughter.*

Before she tumbled into the surf with that one, she made a couple of laps around the breakfast table. She stopped.

"How do I say this without sounding ungrateful?" She wished for the right words. "*Things* are nice. But there's so much more to bringing up a child than presents. All kids really need is love."

"Try filling a growing boy's stomach on that," he said.

"Everyone needs food. A child also needs to be comforted after waking from a nightmare. All the gifts in the world don't mean as much as hearing the words *I love you*." Ella hadn't planned to cry, so the stray tear rolling down her cheek caught her off guard. "I'm sorry. I know my father loved us in his own way. I didn't mean—"

"No, it's fine." Holden said. "Don't be embarrassed about telling me how you really feel. Believe it or not, I might've made the same mistakes as a father. All a man wants to do with a little girl is spoil her."

There was a quiet reassurance to his voice. A dangerous comfort under the circumstances. Ella couldn't afford to let her guard down around Holden and especially since he seemed too intent on keeping her at a distance, except in times like these when he was being her comfort while she was vulnerable.

And then he'd just push her away again.

Ella thought better of it this time.

"I'm tired," she said.

His brows drew together like he was confused.

"We're leaving later, right?" she asked.

"That's the plan." His gaze bounced from her to the screen and back.

Her sense of security with Holden was false. He hadn't opened up one bit. He'd been clear about one thing. She should keep her distance.

"Then I better get some more rest before we leave." She intended to listen this time even if her heart fought her on it.

"I'll think about what you said." Holden glanced up and it was like stepping into sunlight, being bathed in warmth.

"Great. Maybe you'll have this whole situation figured out by the time I open my eyes again." She managed a weak smile as she turned to leave.

"I'm not talking about that," he said. His voice was a low rumble in his chest. "What you said about choices earlier. You might have had a point."

She didn't dare turn around and let him get a good look at her face. She hadn't inherited her father's gift at poker. Her face was easy to read.

And she didn't want to be *this* attracted to Holden Crawford.

Chapter Ten

"It's time to go." Holden's voice was a whisper in Ella's ear. It took a second to register that she wasn't dreaming, and his soothing, deep baritone had her reaching for him. Until she realized she was awake.

"Okay." She pushed up to sitting, keenly aware of the strong male presence next to her on the bed. Thoughts like those were as unproductive as trying to grow grapevines in clay soil.

Ella tried to clear her thoughts. She'd dozed off after an exhausting afternoon. Exhausting because she'd basically done nothing but climb the walls all day and her exchange with Holden had her emotions all over the map.

There was no other choice but to be cooped up and she knew it. Still, she couldn't help but feel like a caged animal and her confusing feelings for Holden intensified everything. Beginning to feel better was almost a curse under the circumstances. She was well enough to move around but they had to keep a low profile or risk endangering Rose. There was no way Ella would knowingly put that sweet old woman in danger.

Every noise had had Ella feeling skittish. Constantly being on alert with no outlet for her energy had caused fatigue.

"I'll wait in the other hall," Holden said. And then she felt his weight leave the mattress. The heat in the room vanished with him.

Ella dressed using only the light from the moon sliding through the slats in the blinds. As much as she didn't want to leave *la hacienda*, putting Rose at risk by staying wasn't an option. And at least she would finally have something to do, a purpose, even if it was dangerous. She'd go stir-crazy if she stayed inside much longer.

Holden was waiting outside the door.

"Ready?" he asked as he took the duffel from her.

"I think so," she said. "Any chance we can wake her and tell her goodbye?"

Ella didn't have to ask to know that Holden had wiped the place clean. The smell of bleach permeated the air.

Her eyes widened at the sound of a motorized vehicle outside. Holden muttered a curse. "Stay right here unless I tell you to come out."

He dropped to the ground and instructed her to do the same. Pain shot up her right thigh at the quick movement. She swallowed her gasp, making no sound as she hit all fours and scooted behind a cabinet.

The kitchen door opened and closed so fast and so quietly it barely registered. Ella was reminded how little she knew about the man who was helping her. Why was he so adept at moving stealthily into the night? Had he served in the military? Or been in law enforcement? The way he'd questioned her earlier gave the impression he might've been. Hadn't he said that he and his father shared similar professions? She wanted to know how it was even possible that her father had met the man. For reasons she couldn't explain and didn't want to analyze, she wanted to know more about Holden.

Another swish of the door and she realized she'd been holding her breath.

"It's all good," Holden said, reclaiming the duffel. He had a second helmet and she figured he must've left it at Rose's on a prior visit.

Ella followed him out the door, surprised at the stabbing pain in her chest at leaving. She'd lost so much already and Rose had managed to wiggle her way into Ella's heart in the short time she'd known her. Rose's eyes belied her smile. There was emptiness there, a hollowness that Ella couldn't ignore.

"I'd like to check on her when I get my life back," she said to Holden. "We have our annual fall festival coming up in a few weeks. Maybe she'd like to come."

"When this is over, you can do anything you want," he said. He wasn't arguing against the idea but he came off like he didn't care either way. Was he reminding her that they'd go on to live their separate lives by then? She couldn't see his face with his helmet on.

Leaving Rose was harder than Ella expected it to be. Her heart broke a little as she climbed onto the back of Holden's motorcycle. She was glad that he didn't notice the tears welling in her eyes at the thought of leaving Rose by herself.

The highway was long and empty when they first started out. Traffic thickened as they headed east and neared major cities. After riding on the back of Holden's motorcycle so long Ella's arms felt like they were being dragged down by hundred-pound weights, they exited the highway.

Holden located a dirt path about a mile off the highway and Ella lost count of how many minutes they'd been on it until he finally stopped.

After Ella climbed off the back of the bike, Holden threw his leg over and hopped off.

"I thought we'd camp for a few days. I have camping gear in my duffel," he said. With his helmet on, visor down, she couldn't read his eyes.

Ella balked. "Seriously? Out here?"

"Sure. Why not?" He removed his helmet to reveal concerned, pinched eyebrows.

"Mosquitoes for one. They'll eat me alive. Showers for another. You won't want to be anywhere near me without one." She was getting nowhere and could tell by his tense expression.

And then his face broke into a wide smile, revealing near-perfect white teeth.

"You think this is funny?" She really was working herself up now and it seemed to amuse him all the more.

"Actually, I do." He turned and walked to a clearing where one of those tiny houses stood. He was jiggling what sounded like keys.

Ella blew out a frustrated breath as she watched him unlock the door.

"Coming?" he asked, and there was a contrite quality to his voice. "Or do you plan to stand out here and become mosquito bait?"

"Think you're funny?" she shot back with a look meant to freeze boiling water.

"I used to," he said under his breath.

And that made her laugh as she walked past him. She couldn't help herself. It was most likely the stress of the past few days and how out of control her life had become, but she laughed.

"I don't know what shocks me more. The fact that you made me laugh or used to think you were funny," she said as he opened the door.

A laugh rumbled from Holden's chest and it was sexy. Ella wanted to shut off her attraction to him. But it felt impossible at the moment. No matter how much she tried to hold it back, she couldn't. So she gave in and it was probably the stress that they'd been under more than anything else, but both of them laughed until she had to sit down.

"That felt good," she said, ignoring the feeling like champagne bubbling up her throat as she wiped tears from her eyes.

"It did." Holden stood at the door, leaning against the jamb, arms folded. "Life used to be…more funny."

"How long did you say you've been living like this?" she asked.

"Twenty-five months." His smile faded.

"That's a long time." She stood.

He nodded and she thought he said, "Too long."

"What about Rose? Will she be safe now that we're gone?" she asked.

"That's the idea. But if they figure out her connection to me…" He stopped as though he couldn't finish the thought let alone the sentence.

"Would she be safer at my family's ranch?" Ella asked. "I could have someone pick her up. No one would have to know."

"She's stubborn." He was already shaking his head. "There's no way she would leave her precious garden for more than a few days."

"What if I talked to her? Maybe she'd listen to me if I came up with a good argument."

"You'd be wasting your breath," he responded.

"It'd be worth a try," she argued.

"You really think you can change people, don't you?" Holden asked, and the question took her off guard.

"Why do you make it sound like a bad thing?" Her defenses flared.

"It's good." He shrugged. "Probably naive. You do realize that you can't save every stray."

"Maybe." She probably shouldn't speak her mind to the one person who seemed intent on helping her. Especially when she was about to send out a zinger. "But at least I don't quit."

That brought an amused smile to Holden's face. "And that's what you think I did?"

"Obviously. You got into trouble and you've been hiding ever since," she surmised.

"I'm sure it looks that simple from the outside." He picked up the duffel and brought it over to one of the chairs. The living room of the place was too small for a couch, but there were two reasonably sized, comfortable-looking chairs with a small table in between. The kitchen was more like a kitchenette with a microwave and a hot plate. Ella's dorm room in college had been bigger, and yet she was never happier to be in a space. There was a full-size bed on the back wall. It would be way too small for a man like Holden Crawford. And a closed door that she assumed led to an equally small bathroom, which was fine because this was so much better than being out there in the elements, exposed.

"How'd you know about this place?" His comments still stung, which meant there was a tiny bit of truth. Ella didn't believe in lost causes. Everyone could be saved. *Except those who refuse help*, a little voice reminded.

"Belongs to a friend of mine." He pulled out the makings for coffee.

She must've balked because he got a defensive look on his face.

"I have friends," he said, defensive.

She wasn't touching that statement. "Are you tired after that long ride?"

"Not really. Riding helps clear out the clutter in my head." He moved to the kitchen and held up a mug.

"Yes, please," Ella said.

"Our conversation is churning through my mind." He heated water on the small stove before filtering the grinds.

"Anything stick out?"

"I just got to thinking about your life, your activities and who might benefit from your death."

"No one, really. The ranch would continue to run. Dad had a trust set up years ago in order to protect jobs in the event something happened to his kids. It's part of the reason his employees were always loyal to him. He looked out for them," she said. "Ed Staples,

"4 for 4" MINI-SURVEY

We are prepared to **REWARD** you with 2 FREE books and 2 FREE gifts for completing our MINI SURVEY!

FREE
Value Over
$20!

You'll get...

TWO FREE BOOKS & TWO FREE GIFTS

just for participating in our Mini Survey!

Dear Reader,

IT'S A FACT: if you answer 4 quick questions, we'll send you **4 FREE REWARDS!**

I'm not kidding you. As a leading publisher of women's fiction, we value your opinions... and your time. That's why we are prepared to **reward** you handsomely for completing our mini-survey. In fact, we have 4 Free Rewards for you, including 2 free books and 2 free gifts.

As you may have guessed, that's why our mini-survey is called **"4 for 4".** Answer 4 questions and get 4 Free Rewards. It's that simple!

Thank you for participating in our survey,

Pam Powers

To get your 4 FREE REWARDS:
Complete the survey below and return the insert today to receive 2 FREE BOOKS and 2 FREE GIFTS guaranteed!

"4 for 4" MINI-SURVEY

1 Is reading one of your favorite hobbies?
☐ YES ☐ NO

2 Do you prefer to read instead of watch TV?
☐ YES ☐ NO

3 Do you read newspapers and magazines?
☐ YES ☐ NO

4 Do you enjoy trying new book series with FREE BOOKS?
☐ YES ☐ NO

YES! I have completed the above Mini-Survey. Please send me my 4 FREE REWARDS (worth over $20 retail). I understand that I am under no obligation to buy anything, as explained on the back of this card.

☐ I prefer the regular-print edition
182/382 HDL GMYH

☐ I prefer the larger-print edition
199/399 HDL GMYH

FIRST NAME   LAST NAME

ADDRESS

APT.#   CITY

STATE/PROV.   ZIP/POSTAL CODE

HI-218-MS17

READER SERVICE—Here's how it works:

▲ If offer card is missing write to: Reader Service, P.O. Box 1341, Buffalo, NY 14240-8531 or visit www.ReaderService.com ▲

BUSINESS REPLY MAIL
FIRST-CLASS MAIL   PERMIT NO. 717   BUFFALO, NY

POSTAGE WILL BE PAID BY ADDRESSEE

READER SERVICE
PO BOX 1341
BUFFALO NY 14240-8571

NO POSTAGE
NECESSARY
IF MAILED
IN THE
UNITED STATES

the family attorney, would oversee it and then he'd name a successor. There are a lot of controls built in so no one can override the document or successfully challenge it in court. I wish I'd paid more attention to that part but I honestly never thought I'd need to know. My dad was such a presence. I just never believed anything bad would happen to him."

Holden paused long enough to make eye contact before continuing. The look seemed meant to be reassuring.

"But we have no suspects and we're no closer to figuring out what happened than we were after the first rock to my head," she said, frustrated.

Holden handed over a mug of fresh steaming brew.

Ella took a sip and mewled with pleasure. "I will never tire of the taste of your coffee."

Her response netted another smile and she liked the way his lips curved.

"You figure out how to make do with what you have in your environment," he said.

"Where are we, by the way?" she asked, realizing it hadn't occurred to ask before now. She'd been too busy laughing and her stomach still hurt.

"We're in Texas," he said.

"I figured that much out," she quipped before taking another sip.

"A couple of hours from Cattle Barge," he said. "I keep rounding back to the fact that we need to be near here in order to track down leads. We might be able to clear this whole thing up if you could talk to people."

"Agreed."

"Don't get any ideas because you can't go back home," he said. "It's too risky and we have to give the sheriff time to do his job. He has more evidence to work with now."

Ella got quiet for a long time. If she could stay alive, Sheriff Sawmill should be able to find the person after her, especially after that last attempt. "I know you make an amazing cup of coffee, and I mean pretty much anywhere with whatever's around. But I don't know much else about you."

Holden's gaze narrowed and his lips thinned, and for a long moment she didn't think he was going to respond. "I told you that I was set up for murder before. Doesn't that make you a little scared to be around me?"

"Why should it? You're innocent." She didn't hesitate.

"I am. But how do you know?" An emotion passed behind his eyes. Hope?

"I've been around bad men before. I'm not as naive as you believe. Dad taught me how to tell the difference a long time ago. Said he was protecting me. When a man's truly evil he has a dead quality to his eyes. A darkness that no light can fill. A man capable of murder, even if it was a passion killing, would have those eyes," she said.

"I was out jogging that morning when it happened," he said after a thoughtful pause. "Came back and found her stabbed to death."

There was an almost-audible thud in Ella's chest at the tight-clipped pain in his voice—pain that he'd held inside for too long. "What happened?"

"As in details? You don't want to know."

"Maybe that's true on some level. You haven't spoken to anyone in more than two years and I think it's time you got this off your chest," she said quietly.

Holden blew out a sharp breath, and for a minute she thought he'd change the subject. There was so much pain behind those pale blue eyes—eyes that had spoken so much to her when she'd first seen them while the rest of his face was buried underneath that beard.

He took in a sharp breath. "Her name was Karen. Blood was everywhere. I bolted over so fast that I didn't even look to see if anyone else was around. Everything moved in beats after that. One beat and I'm standing in the doorway in shock. In the next, I'm beside the bed. My field training told me that pulling the knife out of her chest would make everything worse. Her eyes were already fixed, open... blank."

Ella didn't speak, even when Holden looked like

he might not continue. She just sat there, still, patient. Wishing there was something she could do to help ease his heartache.

"Another beat and I'm trying to stem the bleeding, performing CPR. None of my years in the corps mattered because I couldn't bring her back." He clenched his back teeth. "A few beats later, cops are there. Looking back, that part was strange because I never called them. Guess I just assumed one of my neighbors had heard her screaming. Another beat and EMTs arrived. The whole place was chaos by then. A few more beats and I'm in the back of a squad car being taken in to give my statement, and that should've been my first clue that something was off. Looking back, why wouldn't the cops have had a witness ride in front? And then the cop pulls off on this back road. I had blood all over me, my hands, Karen's blood. I was in shock so it took a minute to register that the cop wasn't heading toward the station anymore. I was in a fog. He orders me out of the back and pulls out his service weapon. Throws a cord at me and tells me to wrap it around my neck."

Holden paused. Ella touched his arm for reassurance. She was listening. She cared about the truth.

"Cop gave me two options. Wrap the cord around my neck or be shot. I told him he forgot my third choice." Holden looked high and away from her like he could see the past there. "Run."

"How did he react?" she asked.

"I dropped down and caught his leg as he tried to shoot me. He went over backward, landed pretty hard and started calling for help on his radio," he said.

"And that's when you got away," she finished.

"My father was tortured and killed a few days later and that's when I knew something big was going on. I still don't fully understand why I was set up to look like a murderer in the first place. I'd only been dating Karen for a few months when the whole thing went down. And, yeah, it was my blade, but I wasn't even in the house when it happened." Holden stared at a spot on the wall for a long moment and she could only imagine the horrors of what he'd witnessed.

"Wouldn't the evidence have cleared you?" she asked.

"If the officers in charge of the investigation had followed it, I would've been fine. They didn't. The officer who took me in supposedly to give my statement never intended for me to live long enough to say what really happened," he said.

Ella gasped.

"Within days of my disappearance reports started showing up about me suffering from PTSD, going berserk and killing my girlfriend and then my father." He made a disgusted face and grunted. "They were so off base and I was angry. But someone important was pulling the strings. Had to be, and I realized how far they would go the minute they killed Pop."

"I'm so sorry," she whispered.

Silence sat between them for a long moment.

"What did you do?" she finally asked.

"At first, I'll be honest. I thought I'd bide my time and then creep back into the shadows. Figure out who committed these crimes. Make them pay with their own lives. The thought of revenge kept me moving forward when I wanted to die," he admitted.

"And now?"

"I remembered a promise that I made to Pop once about looking after Rose if anything ever happened to him. We were fishing and I guess he was getting older. Started thinking about the day he might not be around any longer. She was his only friend when he lost his parents and had to live with a relative in New Mexico. He was kicked around from place to place after that, to whoever would take him. But he and Rose managed to get back in touch," he continued. "She was his North Star and helped him get his life together when it was falling apart. They kept their friendship a secret so none of his relatives knew where to look for him. He'd show up at her parents' place when life got too real and they'd take him in. I guess it never occurred to them to go public with their friendship once they were adults. When I was born and my mom took off, Rose urged him to join the military to straighten himself out. He did.

We moved around a lot before settling in Virginia, where my father established a moving company, but we had each other and we had Rose. Pop might not have been perfect, but he did the best he could, and I respect that in a man."

Ella could relate to those feelings. She and Holden weren't so different no matter how much he wanted to be a man stranded on an island. At least he was talking to her, revealing something about his past and why he was in this predicament. She couldn't imagine walking in to find someone she loved—that word pained her to think about when it came to Holden and another woman—murdered. She shuddered at the thought. And then to find out that your father had been tortured and killed and you'd been blamed. The worst part was that she could see why Holden would hold himself responsible for all of it even though something else had to be going on. Would it really be any different for her?

There was a storm brewing behind Holden's blue eyes as he spoke. He'd lost two people he cared about in a very short time and he held the blame for both. Two long years. So much pain.

"Were the two of you in love?" Ella surprised herself with the question.

"I thought I might have been at the time," he said.

"What changed?" She didn't look at him and scarcely registered that she was holding her breath, waiting for his response.

"My definition."

"How so?" she asked, still not able to look him in the eyes.

"I met you."

He moved into the kitchen and opened the few drawers until he pulled out a pad of paper and a pen. "This'll help."

An hour and a half later, Holden stood in the kitchen reading the long list of Ella's activities. "You're one busy person."

"I already said I was involved in the community," she said, and that solicited a grunt from Holden.

"Involved? Is there anyone else in town doing anything?"

Ella laughed. "I'm sure that I'm forgetting something. Like I said, the days following Dad's death are a little hazy and my head hurts when I try to overthink."

"You mean there's more than this?" He held up the paper. "When do you have time to do anything else?"

"Like what?" she asked.

"Date, for one," he said.

Ella laughed. "It'd be crazy to empty my schedule and wait for Mr. Right to waltz in when there's so much to be done. Besides, I already told you about my personal life."

It looked like a small smile crossed his lips before he took another sip of coffee. "The person who tried to kill you wanted it to look like an accident at first. I'm guessing they were expecting a headline that read Grieving Socialite Falls into Canyon Days after Her Father's Murder."

"Right. But the second attempt was out in the open."

"He could've planned to kidnap you and then set the scene once you were secured. No one had seen you since you'd disappeared at Devil's Lid, so he might've figured that he could kill you and stage it to look like an accident."

"Wouldn't someone notice the bullet holes?" she asked.

"True. The assailant did shoot but that was most likely out of panic."

"Now that I think about it, he shot when I fought him off and ran." She sighed. "Pretty much every household in this part of Texas has a shotgun on property. If not to deter criminals then to shoot predators stalking their herds, so that doesn't help us."

Holden nodded again as he examined the list. "There are a lot of names on here. What about friends? Any arguments with the people in your circle?"

"When do I have time?" she quipped. "I do charity work, which I'm passionate about, and I help run the ranch. I barely have time to eat and sleep."

"That's a choice," he said with a look.

"You're a man on the run and I doubt you've made time for *friends* in the meantime," she quipped. Yeah, she was being defensive. There was something about detailing the boring nature of her private life to a ridiculously handsome man that put her on edge.

Holden held up a hand in surrender. "I make no claim about being perfect. But I have a good reason to stay solitary. Everyone I get close to ends up dead."

She started to argue but he'd made a good point. Had she been pushing people out of her life? Keeping everyone at a safe distance? The short answer? Yes. Never knowing her mother and growing up with an emotionally distant father wasn't exactly the recipe for letting people in. She was as close to her siblings as she could be, but Ella could admit that she'd taken on a mother-like role with them since she was the oldest. At least until the boys were old enough to do what they wanted, and that came early for the independent-minded Butler men. Even now while her life was in danger she was focused on protecting them. Maybe she and Holden had more in common than they wanted to admit.

"Anyone stand out on that list you're holding?" she asked, figuring she'd done enough self-examination for one day. Her brain hurt and that wasn't helping her figure out whatever was pressing against the back of her skull. Something was there but she couldn't reach it, and that was frustrating under the circumstances. The stakes were high and it wasn't like she was trying to remember her shopping list. Trying to force it didn't help, though.

"I'd have to dig around and figure out the impact

these decisions could make to know anything for certain," he said.

"Impossible out here with no laptop or Wi-Fi," she explained. "You already said contacting people is out of the question."

"When my choices are to keep you safe or investigate, I'm always going to choose the first," he said, and there was an emotion present behind his eyes that stirred something primal inside her.

Ella ignored it. Sort of. Her body trilled with awareness.

"We could talk it through over lunch," she said, her stomach rumbling. Had they eaten breakfast?

"I'll head into town for supplies," he said. "I don't like leaving you here alone but it'll be safer for you if we split up."

Holden pulled his Sig Sauer out of his duffel and set it next to Ella.

She glanced at the weapon before locking onto his gaze. "I guess I should've seen this coming. This is the first time I've seen you with a gun."

"I didn't need it before now," he said, and she figured he had a military background by way of his commitment to everything being on a need-to-know basis. "You know how to use it?"

"I have experience with shotguns mostly, but I'll figure it out if I have to," she said with sincerity.

He nodded and that should've been the end of it. He should've walked out the door and gone for supplies.

But he stood there like he couldn't move his feet. It dawned on her why he'd respond that way.

"I'll be okay. Go ahead," she urged. "Nothing will happen to me while you're gone."

HOLDEN WAS SURPRISED at how easy it was to talk to Ella. He'd never had a problem closing up and keeping everything locked inside until her. He shocked himself with the amount he'd wanted to share. He'd been a regular Chatty Cathy back there. He reminded himself to tread lightly. It probably had more to do with the fact that he'd barely spoken to a soul in twenty-five months than the possibility that he could have real feelings developing for someone he'd only known a few days.

Granted, there was something about Ella Butler that gave the impression they'd known each other for years, a familiarity he'd never experienced with another person. She was different from the women he usually dated. But this wasn't the time to get inside his head about it. There were more important issues to think about, like who was trying to ensure she took her last breath. And the issue of him still being on the run after two years in hiding, getting nowhere.

Holden thought about what Rose had told him. The numbers 1-9-6-4 still meant nothing to him and he'd racked his brain during the ride to the small cabin trying to find a connection. He'd first thought it referred to a year and then an address. Nothing came to mind.

Immediately after the murders he'd gone over his last conversations in his head a hundred times, and his thoughts became an endless loop. Looking back from a fresh lens, he thought about his relationship with Pop. How quiet he'd become in those last few weeks before the murders. People talk about intuition all the time. Had Pop sensed something was coming?

Holden parked his motorbike around the side of the country store and purposely kept his sunglasses on to shield at least part of his face. At his height, it was difficult to move undetected and he still felt exposed without a beard. He'd covered his face with one for two years—years that had felt like they'd dragged on for twice that amount.

Ella's words haunted him. Had he given up?

Holden pushed open the glass door and heard a jingle. The chipper cashier looked up from a magazine and welcomed him. He nodded but kept his face turned away in case there was a camera. Seemed like there was one in every store no matter how remote the location. Technology made it more and more difficult to stay off the radar.

He picked up a basket and loaded it with grilling supplies. Normally, he saved steak for a special occasion. In this case, he wanted to feed Ella a decent meal. Based on her devotion to her causes, she seemed like a good person and deserved at least that much.

Her situation haunted him.

The logical answer was that someone had killed Maverick Mike and had now set his or her sights on Ella. The responsible party had clearly wanted to make a statement with Mike's death, but something had changed when the person went after Ella. What? His thoughts kept rounding back to the same thing. *The person.*

He let that thought sit while he approached the cash register.

"This all for you today, mister?" the short brunette cashier chirped. She looked to be in her midtwenties and wore a green shirt and khaki-colored pants.

"Yep." Holden nodded and quirked a smile. He'd found a small gesture like that put people at ease around him. It wasn't difficult to find a smile when he thought about the simple pleasure of grilling a good steak and feeding someone he cared about.

Damn.

Ella's words kept cycling through his thoughts. He'd convinced himself that keeping to himself and staying so far off the grid that he'd become half animal, half man was to keep himself alive until he figured out who was behind Karen's killing. Losing her had been a blow. His father being killed so soon after had knocked the wind out of Holden. It had only been him and Pop since his mother had disappeared not long after he'd been born. Sure, Pop had made mistakes but the two of them had grown up together and Holden could easily forgive the shortcomings. Hell, he was far from perfect himself. When his old man was killed, a piece of Holden had died. His anger had turned inward and he'd retreated to nature, where he'd been trained to survive.

The cashier chirped an amount and Holden paid with cash. He'd cashed out his savings when he went on the run and had kept a low profile, sleeping in vacant cabins and trapping and cooking most of his own food. He took his bags with a thank-you and forced a casual-looking smile.

The cashier beamed up at him. The twinkle in her eyes said she was flirting. Holden wasn't the least bit interested. Being with Ella made him realize how far he'd drifted away from the man he used to be before his life had been turned upside down. That needed to change.

Holden kept his head down as he exited the store. Out of the corner of his eye he saw a white sedan with blacked-out windows fly past and a bad feeling took seed deep in his gut.

He broke into a dead run toward his motorcycle as his pulse galloped. His chest clenched at the thought of anything happening to Ella while he was away. He'd left her with his Sig for protection, not really expecting her to need it. Could she even use it on another human being? A moment of truth like that only came when confronted with the situation. He muttered a few curses after quickly securing the grocery items. He released the clutch and gravel spewed from underneath his back tire.

Ella should never be faced with a kill-or-be-killed situation. Holden should know. He'd had to when he was in the service. And taking someone's life, even an enemy, wasn't something a decent man took lightly.

With the agility of his motorcycle, he caught up to the sedan in no time. As he neared, he heard music blaring. Teenagers?

He whipped around the vehicle in order to get a look at the driver. A strong honk-like sound caused him to look up in time to realize he was about to go head-on with a semi.

Holden zipped around the white car. In his rearview, he could see the driver clearly. He was male and too young to buy a real drink. Relief was short-lived. Holden needed to see Ella with his own eyes and know that she was fine. In the future, he'd figure out a way to take her with him when he left for supplies because being away from her, not knowing if she was safe, did bad things to his mind.

By the time he navigated up the drive, checking several times to ensure no one had followed him, his nerves were shot. She was waiting outside, sitting in the sun, when he parked behind the shack. Seeing her caused a jolt of need to strike him like stray voltage. Holden was done. Done biting down an urge so primal his bones ached. Done holding her back when she'd been so clear that she wanted the same thing. Done protecting her from him. She needed to know that she meant something to him. So he walked right over to her and hauled her against his chest. Her sweet body molded to his. Her fingers tunneled inside his hair as he pressed his forehead to hers. "We can't let this go any further, but I had to hold you."

This close, he could feel her body tremble and need welled inside him. The feel of her soft skin under his hands connected to a life he used to know only this somehow was better. Sexual chemistry crackled in the air around them. Sex couldn't happen but he was done fighting the need to be close to her.

She looked up at him with those cornflower blue eyes and he almost faltered. He reminded himself to keep a grip on his emotions.

"What happened?" she asked.

"There was a car..."

"And you thought it was coming for me," she finished when he paused.

"Yes." He closed his eyes to shut out the other possibilities, the ones that involved him not making it to her in time.

"Are you okay?" she asked, and there was so much concern in her voice.

"I am now," he said, and she didn't seem to need

him to elaborate. She just leaned into him and wrapped her arms around his neck. The movement pressed her full breasts against his chest and for a half second he pictured them naked, tangled in the sheets in a place far away from here.

But that wasn't reality and Holden didn't do fairy tales.

He took in a sharp breath.

"I'll make lunch," he said.

Ella took a step back, away from him, seeming to understand that he needed space. Damn, it was going to be difficult to leave her once this was all over.

For now, he needed to concentrate on giving her her life back. She had plans, meetings and causes to fight for.

What did he have?

A ghost of a life. No family to speak of. Yeah, his life couldn't be more opposite. Another in a long list of reasons he needed to maintain his distance. He would only bring her down.

He was cursed.

Chapter Twelve

Ella smiled as she took another bite of perfectly cooked steak. The potato with all the fixings was just as amazing. "I'm impressed with your cooking skills."

"Don't be. Coffee and steak are all I can do," he said with a crooked smile. She was grateful for the break in tension between them and even more so that her comment brought out a lighter side of him. He looked pleased with himself and like a different person than the one who'd arrived an hour ago. Ghost white with anger written all over his face, Ella could see beyond the mask to the absolute fear inside him.

And then he'd taken her in his arms.

Their sexual chemistry was off the charts and she figured mostly because it felt like death lurked around every corner. The thought that one of them could be gone in an instant when they'd grown to depend on each other solely for survival was odd considering that she hadn't even known the man existed a week ago. Yes, there'd been an instant attraction even before he'd shaved the beard. The feeling had intensified the more time they spent together. A small piece of her—a piece she didn't want to give too much consideration—needed to acknowledge that there was more to their attraction than proximity and circumstance. The rest of her realized that none of it mattered because he carried too much baggage from the past to let it go anywhere. And where would it go? He was wanted for murder and someone was trying to kill her.

When she thought about it in those terms—and really all she could do was laugh—they were quite a pair.

The feeling that something lurked in the far reaches of her mind that she couldn't access frustrated her. She told herself that was the only reason she was preoccupied with her feelings toward Holden.

"What?" he asked, breaking into her thoughts.

"Nothing." She shook her head.

"Whatever it is made you smile and then frown." He set his fork down on his plate. "You should smile more."

If only he knew that she'd been thinking about him.

"It's the food," she lied. "Even if you are a one-trick pony as you claim to be, it's a mighty fine trick."

That netted a genuine smile from Holden. He

should do it more, too. She imagined a life before his world was turned upside down where he laughed easily, held cookouts in the backyard and perfected his coffee-making skills.

"What was your life like before…?" she asked.

He shrugged his massive shoulders. "The usual stuff. Opening-day baseball with Pop in the spring. No matter where we lived we always drove to Queens to watch the season opener."

"What was he like? Your father?" Ella figured Holden would stop her if she touched on a subject he couldn't talk about.

"Quiet. Kept to himself mostly. He and my mother, if you can call her that, had me when they were young. Dear old Mom took off and Pop joined the military after Rose's urging. We moved around a lot, going from base to base. And he was gone for long stretches but the military was family and we managed to get by. Rose was like a mother to me."

"Did your father and Rose ever go out?" she asked.

He shook his head.

"Why not?" Ella toyed with the fork.

"Honestly? I don't know. Pop had feelings for her. I didn't realize that until I was grown, but it's obvious to me as a man." Holden glanced up. "Guess the timing was never right."

"Shame. He sounds like a wonderful man and Rose is amazing. Plus, you would've grown up eating her chalupas." Ella smiled even though her heart dropped when he'd made the comment about timing. It applied to them, too.

"Her cooking skills would've been a definite plus." Holden stood up and she figured that was his way of saying he was done sharing.

Ella had to admit she was surprised at the change in him since visiting Rose. He seemed calmer, more at peace. Rose would've made a great mother.

"Any chance we can go into Cattle Barge safely?" she asked as he offered to take her plate.

"It wouldn't be a good idea," he said as a hint of that earlier fear flashed in his eyes.

"This feels like a stalemate. How are we supposed to make progress if we can't ask people questions or poke around?" Ella followed him inside.

"I've been thinking a lot about that. We could head to San Antonio before sunrise. Do a little digging online at an internet café," he said. "I'd like to make a few calls, too. I might be able to get a little more information from your acquaintances."

"What makes you think that'll help?" she asked.

"I've been thinking about your charity work. We need to see if any of your projects could have had a negative impact on anyone," he said.

"Sounds like looking for a needle in a haystack," she stated.

"It is. But we have to start somewhere and talking about it might help you remember." Holden stretched his long muscular legs. "Have you thought more about those last few days before you went hiking?"

"Yes, but it doesn't seem to be helping. I end up with a headache." She frowned. "Will it be safe for you in San Antonio? It's a big city and people could be watching for you."

"We'll have to play it careful. The murders happened two years ago and in Virginia, so they shouldn't be top of mind anymore. I'd go back to Rose's but that would be too risky for her." He turned on the water in the small sink and hand washed the pair of dishes.

"I know a place we can go in San Antonio," she said. "It's small but has high-speed internet and everything we'd need."

"Any place familiar to you could put us in danger. Whoever is tracking you might know about it," he said. "Since we don't have a clue who is behind your attacks, we don't truly know how close they are to you."

"I could call in a favor from a friend," she said. "I know people who would be loyal to me."

"That may be true under normal circumstances, but believe me when I say a persistent person can break down pretty much every barrier." He wiped water from the plates and stacked them. "Besides, you wouldn't want to put your friends in danger by giving them information that could lead to you."

"I hadn't thought about it like that," she said, realizing that was most likely all he'd thought about since being alone after his girlfriend and father had been killed. The past week had been hell for her being shut out from everything she cared about and disconnected from everyone she loved. She couldn't imagine living like this for two years and especially after losing two people he cared so much about. Other than Rose, they were all he had.

"There's something else," he said. "While we're there I thought it might be a good idea to do a little digging into my past. See what kinds of stories have been running about me since I disappeared. That might give me an idea of who's trying to find me and why. I never could figure out why local police were involved but enough time has passed now that it should be safe for me to surface and dig around."

"I think that's a great idea." Ella managed a smile. When she'd first met Holden, he seemed uninterested in trying to find the truth. His life had become about staying off the grid and surviving day to day. She saw this as progress, good progress toward him reclaiming life.

"We'll grab a motel room in San Antonio," he continued. "See what we can come up with on a computer. I have a few tricks up my sleeve and by the time anyone figures out the IP address, we'll be long gone."

Ella nodded. "When do we leave?"

"Now," he said.

"MIND IF I stretch my legs before we sit on that bike for a few hours?" Ella asked, those cornflower blue eyes breaking down his walls.

"Not as long as I can go with you. I can use a walk," he said. Food was done, dishes were handled and he'd wiped the place clean of fingerprints. He had no intention of letting her out of his sight again after the sedan incident.

"It feels like we're a long way from answers." Ella started toward the trees and he followed.

"Which is why we have to change our approach," he said. Part of him wanted to hunker down right where they were and take a minute to catch his breath. Their luck wouldn't last forever. Ella Butler was big news and it seemed like everyone had a camera and a social media account ready to post news in a few clicks. He couldn't leave her alone and taking her with him to get supplies was risky. In the late-August Texas heat she wouldn't survive for long, and if he took her completely off the grid, they wouldn't know when it was safe for her to come home. Unlike him, she had a life worth returning to. Was that the reason he felt especially drawn to her? It had been so easy for him to disappear. There was no one counting on him, no one expecting him to come back. No one except Rose, Ella would argue. She'd be right, too. He hadn't realized what this was doing to Rose until he'd seen the worry lines etched in her face.

As for Ella, she deserved to get back to her ranch

and the land she loved so much. She was doing important work whereas he'd felt like a drifter since returning to the United States from the action overseas. Time had provided perspective and, looking back, he could see that he'd kept everyone at arm's length. Maybe his and Karen's relationship could've gone somewhere if he'd let her in. But that only made the guilt worse. She'd died because she'd been in his home at the wrong time. Holden knew there'd been a cover-up, but why? Questions he hadn't allowed himself to ask in two years started surfacing.

"Where are you from originally? You don't have an accent, so I can't place you," Ella said, breaking into his heavy thoughts as they walked.

"I'm from everywhere," he supplied.

She shot him a look.

"Military brat," he said.

"I already know that. You had to have been born somewhere," she countered.

"Colorado Springs," he said.

She responded by cocking an eyebrow.

"It's the truth," he said, holding his hands up in the universal sign of surrender.

She increased her pace, moving farther from the tiny house that had felt like a temporary home. A little voice said it felt like that because of Ella.

"What?" he asked. "Am I doing it again?"

"Doing what?"

"I already told you that it's been a while since I've

had a real conversation with another human being. I also plainly stated that I'm no good at it to begin with—"

This time her hands came up to stop him.

"You're doing better than you think," she said. "I wouldn't even be alive right now if it wasn't for you. Thank you for everything you're doing for me. I can see that it's taking you out of your comfort zone and putting you in danger and I just want you to know that I appreciate it."

Holden stayed quiet for a long time. A thousand thoughts raced through his head. He finally settled on "You're welcome."

Ella swatted at a bug as she stomped ahead with a smile. "Did you spend much time in Colorado?"

"Not really. We moved every couple of years, so I never really got attached to one place," he continued.

"That must've been hard in high school." She glanced at him.

"I managed to get out with a diploma. Although I'm not sure how. I got into trouble. Guess you could say I was a brat." Holden grinned.

"I doubt it," she said, rewarding him with another small smile that was sweet and sexy at the same time. "At least this partly explains why you're so self-reliant."

"All my self-reliance can make me difficult to get along with," he warned, and she immediately made a sound.

"I have noticed that you can be—"

"Stubborn."

"Determined," she corrected. "But your skills and knowledge have been useful in keeping me alive, so I'm not about to complain. Even if you can be a little blunt at times."

Holden grunted. "Say what you mean. I'm a jerk."

Ella stopped and turned to look at him. She fisted her right hand and rested it on her hip as she seemed to study his features.

"Are you always this hard on yourself?" She stared into his eyes when he didn't respond. "Never mind. I can already tell the answer to that question. Yes."

"We should get on the road," Holden said. Talking about himself, opening up to another person, was foreign. Especially since it was so easy to do with Ella.

"Okay," she responded. "But first you should know that you always change the subject when I try to talk about you."

"There really isn't much to tell," he said, and she made another one of those harrumph noises that sounded like it tore straight from her throat.

"I could probably write a book about your experiences," she said. "And I'm pretty sure the least exciting thing in your life would be more thrilling than anything I've ever done."

Holden caught her stare and intensified his gaze.

"I could tell you everything about my past. But then I'd have to kill you."

Silence stretched on between them in a checkmate. Until Holden burst out laughing and then she did, too.

"You didn't believe that load of nonsense, did you?" he teased as she swatted his arm.

"Only because I know you were in the military and I assume most of what you did there is classified," she said.

She reached out to swat him again and he caught her hand in his, ignoring her delicate, silky skin.

"At least you know I have a sense of humor now," he said, figuring touching her had been another mistake. His were racking up. He hoped it wasn't a mistake to dig into the past, too. This was the first time in two years he could let himself hope to find answers and bring justice to the person behind the murders.

"You call that funny?" She withdrew her hand.

"I thought it was," he said.

"You really have been alone for a long time." She looked indignant right before her face broke into a wide smile. "See. I can do it, too."

Holden didn't hold back his laugh. "We should head back and then get on the road."

"Think I can check in with my family again?" she asked. "Might be able to fill in the gaps in my memory."

His first response would be *hell no*. But the sorrow mixed with hope in her eyes made him think twice.

"We'll look online first. If anything happened to one of your family members, it would be news," he said. "And then we'll play it by ear."

He wasn't exactly promising her contact but knowing everyone was okay would ease some of her stress. He wanted to give her that much.

She twined their fingers and he didn't stop her even though alarm bells sounded off at her touch.

The campsite wasn't more than twenty yards away. As they neared the clearing, Holden heard noises. He stopped and listened, squeezing Ella's hand to catch her attention. He motioned for her to crouch down and then bit back a curse.

Moving stealthily along the tree line, Holden kept diligent watch ahead. Had the teens been a cover, or had they alerted someone to his and Ella's presence? His friend who owned the place wasn't coming back. As they neared, he heard banging on the door.

"David?" an unfamiliar male voice said. "Are you home?"

Holden navigated him and Ella around the woods so that they could get a look at the front door. Branches snapped as Ella moved and that would give them away to a trained ear. No way was he separating the two of them no matter how much noise she made. As it was his heart pounded his rib cage and all his muscles chorded, thinking someone might've found them.

Moving through the underbrush, Holden positioned

them so that they could see the front door. A male figure, thin, wearing dress slacks and a collared shirt with short sleeves stood there. He was holding something in his hands and had to reposition it, balancing the bundle against his arm and side in order to free his hand and knock.

The situation looked innocent enough but Holden wasn't taking any chances when it came to Ella. He held her hand and watched for suspicious activity from the intruder.

After a few more rounds of knocking without an answer, the older man set down the bundle and reclaimed the driver's seat of his vintage Ford pickup. A minute later, there was only dust settling along the drive.

Holden waited just in case the old man returned.

When enough time had passed, he stood. "Stay right here until I give a signal."

"Who was that?" she whispered, her eyes wide.

"Probably a neighbor thinking that David had come home, but I need to check the contents of that package before you get anywhere near it." His tone was emphatic.

"What if something happens to you, Holden? Where does that leave me?" She made a good point. Without him, she had little chance of survival.

"Okay. Together." He linked their fingers and realized immediately that she was trembling. He never would've known she was scared based on her calm exterior. Ella Butler knew how to put on a brave face.

Holden picked up a branch and moved slowly toward the package, measuring his steps carefully. "We treat this like a ticking bomb, okay?"

"Got it," Ella replied. Her palm was sweaty, so he gave her hand a squeeze for reassurance.

"We'll be fine." He moved with precision toward the object. As he neared, he saw the small box filled with what looked like produce. Brightly colored apples, bananas and zucchinis peeked over the rim.

Holden maintained as safe a distance as he could. He didn't specialize in bombs but it didn't take a specialist to know being this close to one wasn't the smartest idea. He tossed a stick at the box.

Thankfully, nothing happened.

"We're good," he said. But they weren't. Just because they'd dodged a bullet this time didn't mean they would the next.

Holden needed to keep that thought close to his heart as they moved into a more densely populated area.

Nowhere was safe.

Chapter Thirteen

The motel not too far from State Highway 151 was sparse but had all the basics—two beds and a decent shower. The best part was that they could pay with cash and Holden seemed to have more than enough to cover the bill.

"I hope you'll let me repay you for all of this," Ella said, grateful for clean clothes, hard walls and a shower. With Holden, she never knew what to expect, and she could admit there was an excitement about that.

He shot her a look that said he wouldn't.

She started to argue but he brought his hand up.

"I haven't done much of anything for anyone for the past twenty-five months, so no arguments," he said with a tone that said it wouldn't do any good to protest.

And on some level, she understood. She would figure out a way to thank him because he'd gone above and beyond anything she could ever expect.

It was a foreign feeling being on the other end of someone's kindness. Ella had always been the one taking charge and thinking of everyone else. Maybe she could take what she was learning back to the ranch with her and allow others to do more to pitch in. It had felt like the weight of the world rested on her shoulders her entire life.

"The guy at the front desk said there's an internet café a couple of miles from here open until 2:00 a.m.," he said.

"What kind of place is open that late?" she asked almost to herself as she pulled her hair off her face and into a ponytail. It was barely dark, so without looking at the clock Ella knew that it must be after eight o'clock.

"We'll see."

THE PLACE WAS actually a hookah lounge. The atmosphere was perfect for going unnoticed. It was dark inside and surprisingly not as smoky as she'd expected. There were small round tables with pillows on the floor. And the place was filled with what looked like college-aged kids who were chatting in between taking puffs off the hookahs positioned in the center of their tables. Ella had never been to one before but she knew others who frequented them in college. Come to think of it, Ella hadn't done much socializing in the four years she'd attended university, and she'd gone to a state school legendary for its parties. She'd never once thought about letting loose and having a good time. Her life had been filled with purpose and she'd always been an overachiever. A thought struck. Had she been trying to find her worth in being the perfect student? The perfect daughter? The perfect sister?

The revelation caught her off guard. She loved the ranch but had she thrown herself into her job so that she could win approval from her dad? The realization knocked her back a step mentally.

"How many?" the hostess said with a smile, interrupting Ella's thoughts. The young woman, maybe twenty, had beautiful dark hair and wore a jeweled dot on her forehead. She batted long dark lashes at Holden and Ella bristled.

"Just the two of us," he said, then added, "and we'll need access to a computer."

She smiled up at him, a mix of courtesy and flirting. Couldn't she see Ella standing right there? Technically, she and Holden weren't a couple, but this woman didn't know it by the looks of them. They *could* be a couple and this woman was being rude.

"Follow me," she said with a silky voice.

Ella rolled her eyes.

Holden laced their fingers and she noticed he was scanning the room as they walked, a sobering reminder of the danger they were in being out in public. Suddenly, she felt silly for being jealous of the hostess. Was that what she was? Jealous?

Ella sighed sharply.

It had been a long week. She was fatigued and sad and had had a personal revelation that still had her mind spinning. Honestly, she was scared no matter how much she didn't want to own up to it. The nightmare that had started with her father's murder and extended to her present situation wouldn't end and it felt like the stakes were growing with every passing day.

"How's this?" the hostess asked, beaming up at Holden.

"Fine." He barely seemed to notice that she was standing right next to him inside his personal space. Most would consider that rude but Ella decided that it was a cultural thing and not meant to rile her.

"Can I get you anything to drink?" Her gaze dropped to their linked hands and her smile faded just a touch.

A satisfied smile crept across Ella's lips.

"Water for now," he said. "We'll order off the menu after she's had a chance to look over the options."

"Fine," the hostess said before giving Ella a quick acknowledgment and then disappearing.

Ella took a seat at the bar stool facing the wall. Holden glanced around and mumbled something. Best as she could tell, he didn't like the idea that their backs were to the door. He repositioned the chairs so that they could both easily see the screen.

His was more to the side, positioned so that he could keep watch on the door.

Holden handed Ella a menu.

"An Americano sounds fantastic," she said, referring to a shot of espresso topped off with hot water.

"We should probably order something for that," he motioned toward the hookah.

Ella scanned the menu. "Sour apple sounds good."

The hostess returned with two glasses of water. Holden relayed their hookah and drink orders—his was strong black coffee—and then he waited for Ella to make a decision on food.

Everything on the menu looked amazing, or maybe Ella was just starving.

"Gyro sandwich," she finally decided.

Holden ordered the same.

The hostess nodded, gave a curt smile and scribbled down their orders on a small pad of paper.

"Do you remember having any arguments with anyone, specifically during any of your meetings?" he asked as soon as the hostess disappeared.

"I honestly can't say anything sticks out. I mean, people fight back all the time over personal gain. It feels like there's something right there—" she motioned toward her forehead "—but every time I think too hard, I get a headache."

"Effects from the blow you took. If I'd been there five minutes sooner I could've saved you all this," he said with a look of frustration. He might've been able to interrupt whoever did this to her but he would've exposed his presence and put himself in more danger, so she was glad that he hadn't in some respects.

"I've been thinking about the shotgun," he said. "Most people have one beside the bed."

"Which means it could've been anyone," she said.

"Exactly."

"Why is that a good thing?" she asked.

"Because it means we're not dealing with a professional. The guys after me would use a Glock or a weapon that is more precise. I would never see them coming because they wouldn't have to get close enough to hit the mark. They're skilled shooters whereas the person who shot at you couldn't hit you at close range," he surmised.

"Okay, but what about one of my father's exes?" she asked.

"I've been thinking about that," he admitted. "The person who killed your father wanted to make a statement. That could indicate someone angry, vengeful. So, the person kills him and wants everyone to know how mad he or she is. Hurting you doesn't have the same impact because your father wouldn't be around to see it."

"Meaning if this was a revenge killing against my father, they'd save him for last?" she asked.

"Yes," he said. "The first attempt on your life was meant to look like an accident, like you fell and died."

"He goes back to find a body and doesn't. So he

sets up and waits," she said. "But the second time around he doesn't care because he figures I'm going to turn him in."

"At that point, he just wants to get rid of you," he said. "He figures that he's got nothing to lose because if you make it to the sheriff, you turn him in. Think you can remember anything about the man in the mask? Height? Weight?" Holden's fingers went to work on the keyboard.

"If my brain will cooperate, I'll do my best." Ella stilled when the hostess returned.

"Do you have a sheet of paper and a pen?" Holden asked, pulling out his wad of money and peeling off a twenty.

"I'll find something in the manager's office," she said, taking the offering with a grateful smile. Ella was pretty certain the woman winked. Wasn't there a waiter in the place? Why did the hostess have to keep coming back? And she did return not two minutes later with a pad of paper and a pen. When she handed the offering to Holden, she brushed her fingers against his arm.

Ella was starting to see red.

"Excuse me," she said curtly. "Those are for me."

Holden gave her a bewildered look. Surely he hadn't been off the grid so long that he didn't recognize when a woman was practically throwing herself at him.

The hostess walked away with a frown.

"I can't believe how rude that woman is being," Ella said.

A quick glance at Holden burned in her belly because he must've caught on and now he was smirking.

"All I'm saying is that it's bad manners to be so obvious," she defended. "And we don't need the distraction with everything else we have going on."

"Are you jealous?" he asked. "Because I'm fairly certain the woman was trying to be nice."

Ella's gaze caught on the ten-digit number scribbled across the top of the page along with the woman's name. She held up the notepad. "And what do you think this is doing on here?"

A bemused Holden broke out into a smile. "Guess you were right."

"I'm not blind," she said. "And she was being so obvious."

The door opened behind her and Holden's smile disappeared. Ella followed his gaze and saw a lively group of college-aged kids walk inside. Holden's relief was almost palpable and this was a good reminder of the tension.

"I don't like putting all these kids in danger with our presence," he said, demonstrating once again that he put others first. Holden might see himself as selfish but she wished that he could see the real him, the man she saw.

"I don't either," she agreed.

"Let's speed things along so we can get out of here." Holden motioned toward the screen in front of them. His left thigh was positioned on the outside of her right, effectively providing a barrier between her and everyone else. The denim material of his jeans against her leg sent volts of electricity at the point of contact.

He did it without thinking, with such ease, yet the dark circles cradling his eyes told another story. He must be exhausted even if he'd never admit it.

Ella tried to ignore the sexual magnetism pulsing between them with contact. When the hostess returned with food she seemed to pick up on it, too. She shot an embarrassed look Ella's way.

At this point, she was too hungry and worried to stress over a little flirting. Holden was a gorgeous man, tall, built like a brick wall, but his body didn't feel like one. When her skin was pressed against his it was the feeling of silk over steel. He was sex appeal and masculinity and resourcefulness wrapped together in one seriously hot package.

A dangerous package.

HOLDEN DRUMMED HIS fingers on the keyboard and then hit Enter.

Maverick Mike's murder still pervaded the headlines.

"My brothers and sister seem to be safe." Ella sighed. "Nothing is going on at the ranch."

Holden entered a new search, using only her last name.

"What's this?" she asked, scanning the stories. "Two men have shown up in town claiming to be heirs."

"Looks like your long-lost brethren are giving interviews," Holden said, pulling up the site running the stories.

"He looks nothing like us," Ella said of the first person who popped onto the screen.

"The amount of money your father owns will bring out a lot of crazy," Holden said, watching as the man claimed Maverick Mike had had an affair with his mother that had produced a son, him. The journalist conceded that the accuser had declined a DNA test to confirm.

The second accuser agreed to a test, but only on his terms. He said he'd bring in his own, whatever that meant.

"I'm pretty sure these guys aren't being taken seriously," Holden said.

"Could either one of them have tried to kill me?" she asked.

"Anything's possible. Your father has enough money that even if it was divided between either or both of these yahoos there'd be more than enough to go around," he added. "I doubt they'd target each of you individually if they wanted to take it all. They'd most likely set a bomb and take all of you out at once. But then that would be too easy, as well."

Ella shuddered.

"Sorry. It must be strange for a civilian to hear someone talk about life and death so casually," he said. "We got used to it in the military. Doesn't lessen the effect of your actions. But I learned to compartmentalize the missions by becoming numb to the words."

"It's okay," she said but her voice was a little shaky. "I'm just still trying to wrap my thoughts around the fact that any of this is happening. Before my father died, my biggest concern was making sure that I secured funding for the new animal shelter being proposed and now death just rolls off my tongue."

"Do either of them match the size of the man who tried to shoot you?" Holden asked.

"This one is too big. I would've remembered someone who looked like he should be a defensive end on a football field."

Holden's dark brows drew together.

"What is it?" she asked.

"You didn't mention the animal shelter before," he said, turning toward the screen.

"I must've forgotten. I don't know if it's from the hit I took or just stress in general," she said.

Holden pulled up a map of Cattle Barge. "Can you tell me where the proposed site is?"

"Yeah, sure." Her look said she had no idea what

he was getting at. She took over, zooming the map into a location east of downtown. "There. Right there."

"What's around it?" he asked. "Anything interesting?"

"Pilsner Lake isn't far." She pointed it out on the map. "We have a cleanup project going on there. People love to use the lake and the adjacent park but don't feel the need to clean up after themselves. We get a lot of debris on the beaches and animals are getting sick off the rusting cans tossed around."

"Whose property surrounds the proposed shelter site?" he asked.

"Mr. Suffolk," she said. "Why?"

"Is he against the building being so close to his property?" he asked.

"Not him so much but his son has been cranky about it. Says it'll be too noisy and bother his father," she supplied. "It won't. He's just being difficult. Old Man Suffolk's house is all the way over here."

Ella pointed to a spot on the west end of the property.

Holden leaned back in his chair and brought his index finger to his lips. "Wish we could talk to the old man."

"I guess that's out of the question given our current situation," she said. "Seems like he and my father butted heads from time to time. I might not be his favorite person but I doubt he'd want me dead."

He nodded.

"Are you the only one pushing this project?" he asked.

"Mainly, I guess. Without my support it wouldn't make it far but none of these initiatives would," she admitted. "There was talk of him selling his property a little while ago but I think that's off the table."

Holden needed to figure out a way to talk to the Suffolk family.

Ella tensed as someone approached from behind.

"Hour's almost up," the male voice said.

"Thanks for the heads-up," Holden said to the waiter.

Holden typed his name and a moment of hesitation struck as he wondered what would fill the screen when he hit Enter.

His mind hadn't strayed from the numbers Rose had given to him, 1-9-6-4. Talking about Pop had reminded Holden how much he loved fishing and camping. It was probably just a random thought but it was sticking in his mind for some reason. Maybe there'd be something to point him in the right direction out of the dozens of articles that had popped up in the search engine along with several pictures of him, most of which were in his battle fatigues. Where'd they come up with those pictures? He scanned the stories, noting the strong emphasis on him being ex-military and considered armed and dangerous. Stories like these would bring out all types of bounty hunters hungry for a reward. In his case, it was substantial. Two hundred and fifty thousand dollars were being offered for his safe return to Hampshire Police. That kind of cash would bring people with guns out of the woodwork to hunt him down. No wonder it had always felt like eyes were on him, like he was constantly being watched.

"That seems high," Ella said almost under her breath.

"It is," Holden agreed. He read other headlines. Ex-Marine/Killer Suffers Signs of PTSD.

If the news affected Ella, she hid it well.

"This is untrue," she said hotly. "I don't know that much about PTSD except that you've been around gunfire and I'm pretty sure you would've had some kind of reaction. You have no nightmares, which I've read are part of it. Plus, all the stress we've been under would've triggered something. You're the most calm and collected man I've ever known."

Her indignant tone brought a wave of relief. Holden didn't want her to believe the lies that had been spread about him. For some odd reason that mattered a great deal.

"I thought journalists had a responsibility to print the truth," she huffed.

He covered her hand with his and she looked at him. Those penetrating blue eyes, the ones capable of seeing past the facade to the real him, searched his face.

"Thank you." His throat dried and he had to resist the urge to lean toward her as her tongue darted across her lips. "Your confidence means a lot."

Her eyes darkened as she held his gaze.

"I've been around you long enough to know this is fiction," she said. "You're kind and giving and nothing like the picture painted with these articles."

Well, hell, those words did it. Holden dipped his head and kissed her moist mouth anyway. She'd just taken a drink of her Americano and tasted like coffee.

He caught someone walking toward them out of the corner of his eye. He put his arm around Ella and turned to acknowledge the figure moving their way. Relief washed over him when he saw that it was the hostess.

"Everything taste okay here?" she asked with a glance toward the hookah pipe.

Holden didn't acknowledge the irony there.

"Perfect." And he meant that about Ella. She was the most giving person he'd met. She'd grown up with every privilege but it didn't show. She was down-to-earth and put others' needs first.

The hostess smiled and told them to call for her if they needed anything else.

Holden picked up the mouthpiece as he thanked her. They didn't have to smoke but they did need to put on a better show. He touched it to his lips and then handed it to her. She did the same.

"We should eat," he said as soon as the hostess was out of earshot.

Ella's plate was cleaned and her mug was drained ten minutes later.

"Maybe I can call the sheriff and see if he found any evidence at the scene," she said.

"There should be shell casings," he agreed.

"Is it risky to call from here?" she asked.

"We'll pick up a throwaway phone at a convenience store tonight on our way out of San Antonio. That way you can call in the morning when we're on the road. We'll set out north, make the call and then double back south once you find out what else the sheriff knows," he said.

"He might've solved the case by now and we wouldn't know." Ella motioned toward the screen.

"Are you kidding? You and your family are news." His fingers pounded the keyboard and she saw that he was typing her name.

Socialite Believed to Be Dead read the headline. She stared at the screen. The article went on to say that a substantial amount of her blood had been found at the scene of a shooting and a blood trail ended in neighboring bushes. The suspect was still on the loose. The last line in the article read that her body had not been located and the sheriff's office wouldn't close the investigation until he found answers.

"I spoke to Sheriff Sawmill. There's no way a

story like this should run. Why would he say something like this?"

Holden studied the screen. "The way this article reads, the journalist suggested you were dead and the sheriff didn't correct him or her. I'm sure he has reasons for allowing the public to buy into that nonsense."

"May must be worried sick. She reads the paper every day," Ella said. "I can't even imagine what the others in my family must be thinking, my friends."

"We'll get word to May. Let's hope the others aren't watching the news," he said.

"They probably aren't. They've been avoiding the media and I'm sure they won't want to read all the stories that will come out about our father." Ella's gaze narrowed. "I'll never believe another thing I read online again. I had no idea there were so many lies and untruths."

"Agreed. And I don't like seeing this any more than you do, but this is good news for us," Holden said. "The person responsible for the attempts on your life will most likely let his guard down now."

"What if he's smarter than that?" she asked. "What if he realizes that I'm alive and is waiting for me, biding his time?"

"This guy makes a lot of assumptions and mistakes," he stated.

"True." She seemed to catch on to what he was really saying, that if this guy was any smarter, she'd already be dead. "Think we can go back to Cattle Barge if I put on something to cover up my face?"

He remembered why fishing with Pop had stuck in his mind a few minutes ago. Rose had mentioned his father bringing up fishing. It might mean nothing but Holden wanted to explore it anyway. There was a place the two of them always returned to. Maybe something was there?

"There's something I need to do in Colorado first," he said. "We need to go there before we do anything else. I need to look through my father's personal items. My father gave Rose the message 1-9-6-4 for a reason, and we might find answers in his belongings. Are you good with that?"

"I'm all in, Holden."

Chapter Fourteen

"I think my arms are actually going to fall off." Ella gladly climbed off the back of the yellow-and-chrome motorcycle. She shook her hands and wiggled her arms, trying to get blood flowing again. They'd stopped off every few hours on the ride to Colorado for coffee and snacks but hadn't slept.

Holden took off his helmet and cracked a smile that didn't reach his eyes. "You didn't enjoy the open road?"

"I've been on the back of that bike more than I ever want to be on the back of anything ever again. I don't even think I could get on another ATV now." Ella bit back the urge to complain about the fact that they were in a remote area. Granted, it was beautiful. The landscape was filled with dogwood, birch and towering oak trees. She recognized the scent of Douglas firs and it made her think of Christmases back home with her dad. Her heart ached at the thought she would never get to spend another holiday with him. Sadness overwhelmed her and she had to move. Walking helped her refocus on what needed to be done instead of on the hole in her chest when she thought about her father.

The last road sign she'd read said they were in a town called Newburg. Holden had parked near a shed that looked like it could house a minivan. It was old and looked abandoned from outside appearances. She figured this was the perfect location for hiding valuables. The sun would dip below the mountains soon and darkness was imminent. The small shed didn't look to have any power running to it and there was no sign of a light bulb.

"How long do we have before we run out of daylight?" she asked.

"Not long. I'm hoping that the flashlight app on the throwaway I bought will suffice." He'd bought one of those pay-as-you-go cell phones at a gas station convenience store that couldn't be traced back to him.

"I'm guessing there are boxes or containers in there," she said.

"This is where we used to keep camping supplies." The hollow note to his voice reminded her that he hadn't allowed himself a chance to grieve. Work and staying busy were good for sorrow, but bottling up emotions was dangerous.

Ella couldn't imagine that going through his father's personal items was going to be easy for Holden. She couldn't even begin to fathom going through her father's. She and her siblings would have to face that task at some point and she dreaded it with everything inside her. "What are we looking for?"

"Good question." Holden pulled out a small satchel from underneath the seat of his motorcycle and retrieved a key from it. He unlocked the storage shed and opened the doors. The entire building could house a minivan and that was about it.

Boxes were stacked floor to ceiling with a little room for walking to the left. The two of them wouldn't fit inside, not with Holden's sizable build. The idea of climbing in there with spiders and possibly field mice made Ella shiver, so she would let Holden do the honors.

"You don't have to go in there." Holden stood there, looking like he wasn't quite ready to cross that threshold either.

"I'll be fine. In case you hadn't noticed, I grew up on a ranch." She wanted to spare him but knew there wasn't much she could do.

"Right. I did know that," he said. All humor was gone from his eyes and he looked like he was staring at a ghost.

"We don't have to do this today," she offered. "We could grab a room. I saw a town an hour ago. We could eat and you could have a cold drink."

"We're already here." There was a somber quality to his tone. "We might as well get started."

"Is it safe to be here?" she asked.

"If anyone knew about this place, the boxes would already be gone," he informed.

"I can get a box. Step aside," she cautioned as she moved past him. She was pretty sure something moved in the grass next to her and she almost chickened out until she took another look at his face; his eyes were so intent. Her legs felt like she was walking on rubber bands and her stomach clenched, but she forged ahead like nothing was wrong.

He hesitated for a second and then pulled out the first box. "It's light." He opened the top. "Clothes." He picked up a couple other boxes. "Same in here. I doubt we'll find what we're looking for in any of these."

"We can keep going until we find something. I'm sure 1-9-6-4 will make sense when we see it," she said, not sure what *it* was.

"Pop always talked about buying land and building a house in Colorado. He wanted to be closer to Rose so the two of them could keep each other company as they grew old." Holden opened another box. "Maybe he moved some of his valuables here to prepare. He never really talked about retiring but he'd never really talked much about his moving business."

"I'm guessing no one knows about this property," she said.

"Rose would've said something before if she had any idea." He lined up a few boxes on the ground.

Ella began with the one on the end and he moved to the other side.

Carefully, she examined the box for any creepy-crawly bugs that might be lurking inside and especially for anything that might be venomous now that her radar was up.

"We have no idea what we're looking for." Frustration edged his tone.

"We'll know it when we see it," she reassured.

Light had faded and it was hard to see inside the boxes. Ella didn't feel great about sticking her hand inside them in the dark.

"Hold this." Holden held out the throwaway phone.

Ella took it.

"Position it this way," he said, moving her hand.

He moved back to the box he'd been working on. He pulled out two heavy-duty bags by their handles. He set them down in between two tall fir trees.

"What are those?" Ella followed him, positioning the light so he could see what he was doing.

"You'll see." He didn't look up as he unzipped the first and pulled out a bundle.

"That a tent?" Ella had no plans to sleep in there. She hadn't done that since she was a little girl out with her brothers.

"Better. I have a pair of sleeping hammocks." He seemed pretty pleased with himself but they were losing light and her sense of humor was fading along with her energy.

Ella bit back a yawn. Exhaustion made her wish she had toothpicks to prop her eyes open with.

"How tired are you?" he asked.

"There's no end." Her arms had felt like dead weight hours ago on the bike and it would take days to recover.

"You can get some sleep as soon as I get these up." There was no sign of him making a joke.

"You're kidding, right?" She hoped.

"Why? They're still in good shape," he said.

"Because I'll be mosquito food," she stated. "Are there no motels in Colorado? I could've sworn we passed a couple on the highway before our exit."

"Don't worry. These have nets and we'll be safer if we stay away from major roads. No one knows about this place and I have power bars and water in my backpack to keep us from going hungry. They'll get us through the night and morning, when we can finish going through the boxes. We're about to lose light and we should probably save phone battery." He hooked a rope around one of the firs and then secured it with some Boy Scout maneuver she'd seen one of her brothers do when they were kids.

She couldn't argue with his logic. It would most likely be safe for them out here in what felt like the wilderness even if the place did give her the creeps. Living on a ranch was a different beast. Ella was used to wide-open skies after growing up at Hereford. Colorado was beautiful, but it also felt a little claustrophobic with the thick layers of tall trees.

"It'll be good. You'll see," he reassured when she didn't respond.

"I'm sure it will," she said without much conviction. "Want some help?"

He nodded.

Her vision was blurring and sleep, even out here, sounded better than a steak dinner about now.

"Hold here," he said and his fingers brushed hers. He moved next to her and she could feel his masculine presence.

Being out here with no one and nothing besides each other made her miss the ranch. She couldn't remember the last time she'd wanted to leave Hereford, but it had to have been college. She'd gone to state school to be close to home. *Home.* Ella wished she and Holden were there now.

But what was home to him?

She couldn't even imagine this being his life for the past two years. She thought about how alone he must've been feeling, must still feel, being away from everything and everyone he cared about for so long. Two years could seem like an eternity. So much could change.

Holden moved away from her and she immediately felt his absence.

"Thanks for everything you've done for me," she

said. "I realize you have a lot going on with your father's case, and yet you're still helping me."

He waved her off like it was nothing. But it wasn't. And when this was all over she would figure out a way to show her appreciation.

After tying off the ropes and ensuring their hammocks were secure, Holden went to work building a fire. His movements were swift and there was a certain athletic grace to them, his muscles tensed and stretched against the cotton fabric of his sweatshirt.

Ella redirected her thoughts. No use going down that road again, the one that had her attracted to a man whose past would always haunt him.

Although the landscape looked completely different, being outdoors reminded her of home. She sat down in front of the campfire. Everything about Hereford reminded her of her father and, once again, she couldn't believe he was gone. Holding on to her knees, she rocked back and forth.

"EVERYTHING ALL RIGHT?" Holden dropped down beside Ella and handed her a power bar and bottle of water.

"I miss him," she said, and he could see tears streaming down her cheeks in the glow of the campfire. She hugged her legs even tighter. "Everything's been happening so fast that my brain hasn't had time to process the fact that when I go home he won't be there. He's never coming back."

"I'm sorry." Those were the only two words he could think to say and they fell short of what he wanted to communicate.

"He was larger than life. He was just this huge presence. You know? And now there'll be a gaping hole in his place at the ranch," she managed while fighting off sobs threatening to suck her under. "I can't imagine life on Hereford without him, and that's exactly what I'm going back to. A life where he doesn't exist. Going through your father's belongings made me realize that I'll be doing the same thing very soon."

"He sounds like he was a good man underneath it all. I have a lot of respect for him," Holden said. He knew firsthand what it was like to lose a father, and that meant he also knew there was nothing that he could say to take away the pain. Instead of issuing empty words, he put his arm around her and drew her close. She responded by leaning into him.

"He was," she said quietly.

To say the day had been difficult was a lot like saying bears had fur. Being around his father's things brought back all kinds of memories, most of them good. Hell, Pop's clothes still smelled like him.

Being here made Holden feel close to Pop, in a way. Holden remembered the first time his father had taken him fishing. He'd caught a large-mouth bass twice the size of his fist and they'd gone most every weekend until Holden reached the age hanging out with his old man on the weekends wasn't cool. Then they'd gone on holidays like Father's Day and Fourth of July. Forget barbecuing hamburgers—they'd clean the fish they caught and toss them around in batter. They'd fill up on fried catfish until neither could walk. There'd been hard times, too.

Growing up without a constant feminine presence, save for occasionally spending time with Rose, had brought its own set of challenges. Holden couldn't help but notice the similarities between his father and Ella's in that regard. The men were completely different but each did his best to bring up his family.

Despite any hardships, Ella had turned out all right. It couldn't have been easy for a girl to grow up without a mother. Nurses and caretakers only went so far. But she'd grown into a caring, intelligent, giving woman. *Beautiful woman*, a little voice felt the need to remind him. He wouldn't argue. She deserved better than this.

For tonight he was pleased that she had a soft hammock, warm covers and food in her stomach.

THE SOUND OF twigs breaking underneath shoes woke Holden with a start. He glanced around quickly, gaining his bearings. He didn't mention to Ella that black bears can be up to nine feet tall and weigh in at close to seven hundred pounds.

He closed his eyes and listened.

The twig snaps grew louder, indicating that the snapper was heading toward their campsite.

Holden moved into action, swiftly and quietly. He was at Ella's side in a heartbeat, gently shaking her.

Her eyes opened and he said, "Someone's coming. It's okay."

He deliberately said someone and not some*thing*. Startle her and she might panic, drawing unwanted attention toward them. "We need to move away from camp as fast as possible."

She nodded and bolted into action, throwing off the blanket he'd placed on her last night. He handed her her shoes and she put them on and laced them up in a snap.

The sounds were getting closer and this time he heard voices. It was a relief on some note because that meant they weren't about to encounter a bear. However, people often turned out to be far more dangerous than wildlife. Wildlife made sense. They simply followed the natural order and acted according to laws of nature and their DNA's programming. Humans were unpredictable.

"What is it?" Ella whispered, and the sound of her voice first thing in the morning stirred dormant places inside him that he couldn't afford to let wake. Not when everything in his life was uncertain.

"Hikers," he said. "I need to get a closer look to evaluate the threat. I'm not leaving you here alone."

"Okay." She yawned. "Let's go."

"Stay low and close," he said.

He led her into the woods, far beyond the hikers. He wanted to come up on them from a different angle, from behind. And especially so that he could draw them away from camp.

There were two males and a female. They were chatting easily and looked to be in their early twenties. They were dressed like L.L. Bean models and the female had a black bandana tied around her head. Their hiking boots were clean, which meant they'd just been bought or didn't get taken out much.

Holden looked at Ella and whispered, "Follow my lead."

She smiled her response.

He took her hand, stood up straight and said, "It's chillier this morning than I expected even at this altitude."

"I know, right?" She beamed at him as he made an effort to stomp through the underbrush toward a path. "Brrr."

"Oh, hey. Morning," Holden said to the trio as he and Ella approached.

"Morning," the female said as the guys nodded and smiled. She had dark hair in twin braids running halfway down her torso. Up close, the guys looked to be nineteen or twenty at the most. His estimate of the group being college coeds seemed to be spot-on.

"Been up here long?" he asked.

"Aiden had the bright idea to wake up at four this

morning," one of the guys said. "I'm Patrick, by the way. And this is Keisha."

Holden shook hands with each of the guys and then Keisha offered her hand. The group exchanged perfunctory greetings before Holden laced his fingers with Ella's.

"We ran into a park ranger a mile or so back. He said to watch out for black bears. A big one was spotted heading south," Holden lied. He pointed almost directly toward camp.

Ella's hand tensed. She must not have considered the possibility of bears last night, and that was probably for the best. Holden had learned that being stressed about danger didn't make it go away. Stress was an unnecessary distraction on a mission. All a man needed was enough fear to keep him sharp and give him a clear mind and the confidence that he could handle whatever he faced.

Damn, it dawned on him that he'd strayed far from the one philosophy that had kept him alive through countless missions as a marine. As soon as he figured out what the men after him wanted and who was ultimately behind the murders, he had every intention of reclaiming his life.

"How big?" Keisha asked.

"Maybe eight feet tall and close to six hundred pounds," Holden stated.

"Thanks for the heads-up, man," Aiden said with

wide eyes as he repositioned his body east. "We'll keep watch."

"The ranger said we should make a lot of noise," Holden added.

"Cool. Good idea." Patrick paused, his gaze landing on Ella. "Do I know you?"

"I doubt it," Ella said a little too quickly, giving away her nervous tension.

Patrick's eyebrow shot up as he studied her face. "I know I've seen you before."

Chapter Fifteen

Holden squeezed Ella's fingers for reassurance. All she had to do was breathe and she'd be fine.

"I'm not from around here," she clarified, and that seemed to satisfy the coeds for the time being.

They turned to face the same direction as Patrick.

"Wouldn't hurt to find a big stick and carry it with you just in case you run into that bear," Holden said, turning in the opposite direction, west.

"Thanks for the tips," Patrick said. His gaze was fixed on Ella. "I could swear that I've seen you before. Have you been on TV?"

"Me? TV?" She shook her head and laughed. "Nah."

Patrick seemed to accept the answer but the puzzled look stayed on his face. He was scanning his memory for where he'd seen her before and that wasn't good.

"Keep watch out for that bear," Holden reminded, trying to distract Patrick.

"You got it. You, too," Patrick said before shaking his head and refocusing on his group.

When the trio disappeared, Ella exhaled.

"That was close," she said. "I almost panicked."

"You were fine," Holden reassured her, wanting to give her confidence.

"I thought I almost blew our cover," she continued as he redirected their movement toward base camp.

"We deflected them for now but there could be more hikers, and since your face has been splashed all over the media we can't be too careful," he said.

"Right," she agreed.

"So, we find what we came for and get out of here before we run into anyone else." Holden located a walking path.

"I thought your dad owned this land," she said. "Why not just kick people off?"

"First of all, I didn't want to attract any more attention to us than we already had. And this land is very near a hiking trail, so it'd be easy to end up on Pop's property," he clarified.

Back at camp, he produced a couple of power bars and bottled water. Ella already had her own travel toothbrush that she used after breakfast. Holden made quick work of doing the same and then built a small fire. Ella was already through the first box when he produced two tin cups of coffee.

The idea of going through more of his father's personal effects sat hard on Holden's chest.

"I'll never figure out how you do this so well, but I will forever be grateful that you can," she said with a little mewl that made him think of the similar sound she'd made when the two of them were in bed at Rose's house.

"You learn to make do with what you have in the military."

"Thank you for your service, by the way. I meant to say that earlier," she said, and the reverence in her voice made his chest fill with pride.

"You're welcome." Holden drained his cup and joined her at the boxes.

The ones with clothes had already been stacked next to the storage shed, so he pulled out a few more. One by one they were working their way through them. Nothing stood out in the memorabilia, except the depressing note that the most important items in his father's entire life could fit into a ten-by-twelve-foot shed.

"I thought for sure we'd find something here," he said, doing his best to hide his frustration as he stared at the last couple of boxes. This was turning out to be another dead end and they needed to get on the move again before anyone else stumbled upon the place.

"We've checked everything in these." Ella motioned toward the line of opened containers. There were a couple dozen. "Unless you think there might be something in one of those clothing boxes."

Going through his father's personal effects caused a lump to form in Holden's throat. He could only imagine what it would be like to go through the old man's clothes. His trophies and metals were personal items, but garments were even more so.

"I guess it's worth a try," he agreed.

"We don't know what we're looking for, so how can it hurt?" she asked.

"True."

"This must bring back a lot of memories," she said and there was a sad note to her voice.

"It does," he admitted. "A lot of good memories."

She smiled.

"I just saw something move and I'm pretty sure it's a copperhead." The haughtiness in his voice should've warned her that he was goading her, but she hopped to her feet faster than he'd ever seen lightning strike.

"Where?" She froze, holding perfectly still as she searched the grass.

Hearing Holden's laugh rumble from his chest had her swatting his arm. She drew her hand back pretty fast, and that got him laughing more. It was probably the stress of the last few days that had him needing a break.

"If you want my help, you're going to have to quit giving me a hard time." The pout to her lips made him want to kiss her again.

"Fine. We'll call a truce." He offered a handshake.

She took it.

"No more teasing," he said. "It's just nice to have a normal conversation for a change."

Ella nodded. She shot him a look that said she got it. They both could use a sense of normalcy after everything they'd been through and what they faced ahead.

She dropped onto her knees and opened another box. "Do these make you think about what happened?"

"Yes. At first, I was filled with so much rage. I wanted to track down the men responsible for his and Karen's deaths." Holden paused, fighting back the images of Karen on his bed with blood everywhere and where his imagination always went thinking about what they'd done to his father. Guilt tore into him at the memories.

"What changed your mind?" Ella asked.

"I realized that if anything happened to me, the men responsible would never be brought to justice. I wanted to wait so I could get revenge on my own terms," he said.

"Being angry must come with the territory," she said. "I feel that way now sometimes and I get frustrated. It doesn't change anything. Won't bring back my father."

"Don't be too hard on yourself. From where I sit, you have amazing strength," he stated.

"Maybe from the outside." She pointed to the center of her chest. "In here, I feel like a fragile mess."

"Believe me, you're not." Holden moved to her side and tucked a stray strand of wheat-colored hair behind her ear.

"I wish I was more like you," she stated and it caught him off guard. "You're strong." She glanced at his chest. "And resourceful."

"You think that you're not?" he asked, trying not to let his emotions get the best of him because they had him wanting to pull her close. There was always an undeniable draw toward Ella. Were his emotions getting the best of him being around his father's things?

"I'm nothing like you," she pointed out.

Holden broke into a smile. "That's probably a good thing. I'm stubborn and difficult."

"I was going to say focused and intelligent." It was a good thing she didn't look up at that moment. Holden fisted his hands to keep them from reaching for her.

"You said your dad was into baseball." She held up a card. Holden took a couple of strides toward her. The card was encased in plastic, a collector's edition Hank Aaron. "He was my father's all-time favorite player."

"He's a legend," she agreed.

"You know Hank Aaron?" Holden asked.

"Everybody knows him," she said matter-offactly. And then she rewarded him with a smile. "Plus, I have brothers who were obsessed with baseball."

That made more sense.

"This is the only card in here. The only thing to do with sports at all." She held it up.

A flood of warm memories bombarded Holden as he took the offering. "I haven't even seen a game in years."

"Do you miss it?" Ella asked, and the question caught him off guard.

"I guess I haven't allowed myself to think about it. You get focused and shove everything else out of your mind in order to survive. All you think about is making it through each day."

"There's something perfectly simplistic sounding about that," she said. "No complications."

"Not much of anything. You can't let yourself focus on what isn't in your life." Holden looked at the card. "To do otherwise would ensure a slip."

"You didn't miss home?" she asked.

"Only one place remotely felt like home to me. Your ranch." He didn't look at her. Before he could get too caught up in nostalgia, he reminded himself the longer they hung around the more danger they were possibly in. They needed to stay on the move and they needed to get going.

"I'm glad you found me, Holden," Ella said.

"Yeah?" he asked.

She nodded. "Not just for the obvious reason that you saved my life. I mean that I'm glad it was you who found me."

He offered a smile. He was, too. He pocketed the card, hoping that keeping it with him would make him feel somehow closer to his father. The past two years had been about trying to forget. It was time to remember. Everything.

"I'd forgotten about how much Pop loved his favorite player," he said appreciatively.

"It was in there all by itself, so I thought it might be important to him." Ella went to work on another box.

Holden dug into the clothing box in front of him and his hand hit something hard. He felt around and realized it was metal. It was the size of a small cash box but sturdier. He pulled it out.

"What is that?" Ella stopped what she was doing and moved beside him.

Holden played with the heavy metal in his hands. "Some kind of lockbox."

He looked around for something he could use to break it open.

"I'm guessing you don't have the combination." She examined the strongbox along with him.

"All I need is a crowbar." He didn't have anything close on hand.

Ella disappeared inside the shed. "There's nothing in here."

Holden picked up a rock and Ella shivered when she got a good look at it.

He set the box down and dropped the rock. Nothing happened. Not even a dent. Holden dropped down to his knees and slammed the hard edge again and again against the box. Nothing.

"My dad has a few things like that at the ranch. He uses our birthdays as combinations." She pointed to the numbers on the side.

"Here goes." Holden entered his birthday.

More nothing.

Except voices. Holden listened. It was the trio from earlier and their voices were drifting up.

"Let's clear out," he said. "We'll take this with us and play around with it once we settle into a motel."

Side by side they took down the hammocks and replaced the moving boxes.

"Where are we going next?" She looked up at him with bright, trusting eyes after he closed and locked the doors.

"I plan to find a hot shower and a soft bed for our next stop," he said.

"That sounds like heaven." She clucked her tongue. "Actually, better than heaven. But I'm grateful that I got to brush my teeth this morning."

"Little things like that make a huge difference when you've lost everything," he agreed, securing the strongbox on the back of his motorcycle.

"They really do," she agreed. And then she took

one look at the bike before shaking her head. "I don't think my body will allow me to get on the back of that thing again."

"It would take a lot longer to hike down the mountain, but we can if you want," he offered.

She eyed the motorbike and then the woods. "Were you kidding about black bears earlier?"

"Afraid not," he admitted. "We can do like I told the others and make a lot of noise on our way down. Believe it or not, those bears don't want to be around us any more than we want to run into them."

"As much as that may be true, we can't walk all the way back to Texas," she said on a sigh.

"I have a surprise waiting," he said. "If you can make it down the mountain."

"Then I'll get on the back of that thing again," she said, and he almost laughed at the sound of dread in her voice.

He handed over her helmet. At least it shielded her face. Especially when she put the visor down.

"If I end up with bugs in my teeth, I know who to blame," she said as she climbed on behind him.

"I'll take the hit for that one. Just don't smile," he quipped. Despite himself, Holden laughed and it was good to get a break from his somber mood. Going through Pop's things proved more difficult than Holden had expected, but having Ella there made it tolerable. He'd forgotten what it was like to have real companionship with someone he cared about, partly because he'd never connected with someone like he did with Ella. Yeah, he cared about her. He'd fallen down that rabbit hole. Couldn't say he was especially sorry either.

Talking to Ella was easy and he was starting to enjoy the way they bantered back and forth. This was real conversation and the closest he'd come to talking about something normal in two years. Before her, he didn't realize how much he missed it. Or course, he couldn't deny that he liked talking to her more than he'd ever liked talking in general. In fact, he didn't remember being all that into conversation before spending time with her. Few people made him laugh. Fewer got his sense of humor and laughed with him.

There was something special about Ella Butler.

ELLA LET OUT a yelp of excitement as she followed Holden into the standalone garage and stood in front of the sport-utility vehicle.

"This is our ride?" she asked. "Are you serious?"

"Belongs to a friend of mine who said I could take it anytime I needed to," Holden said. "I figured this was as good a time as any to take him up on it."

"Won't he miss it?" she asked.

"He would if he was in the country." Holden moved to the workbench in the detached garage. "As for now, he's a contractor for the US military and living in Jerusalem."

"You're sure he won't be upset?" She clapped. She couldn't contain her excitement any more than a kid could refuse an ice-cream cone on a hot summer day. This was just as good. It would have AC and doors and a real seat. The banana-like wedge on Holden's motorcycle had her bottom completely numb after an hour.

"Are you kidding? He'd insist." Holden felt along a wooden workbench before his hand stopped and he came up with a set of keys.

"We won't be putting him in danger, will we?" The last thing she wanted to do was involve anyone else in their problems.

"None that he wouldn't welcome if he were state-side," Holden said. He jangled the keys. "Ready?"

"Am I?" she said. "Are you kidding? I could kiss you."

Those last words hung in the air and had come out completely on impulse.

"I didn't mean," she started to say, but words were pretty useless. Her cheeks felt like they were on fire.

"Don't be embarrassed," he said. "I want you to feel like you can relax around me."

"I got a little too comfortable," she said along with an apology. "Because I wasn't joking."

"Don't be sorry," he countered.

"The problem is that I do want to kiss you, Holden. And that's not where we need to be right now," she said and walked to the passenger's side.

She didn't exhale until the SUV blocked her view of him. It was true. She liked kissing him. And where would that get either one of them? They were on the run and their heightened emotions were running away with them. Realistically, Holden would move on as soon as she was out of danger. Sure, they had chemistry. That was obvious. But real feelings?

Ella couldn't even go there. Not with him. Not with anyone. Not until she sorted out her life and got a handle on the property. Once she was clear of this danger, she'd go back to her life on the ranch, her charity projects. That life made sense to her. This, being on the run with a magnetic roamer wouldn't last. He'd get bored and move on.

Besides, Holden was in love with a ghost and Ella couldn't compete with that. Not to mention the fact that neither had a future at the moment. She expected him to unlock the door but he didn't. Instead, he came up from around the back of the SUV.

"Where should we be?" he asked, and there was so much torment in his voice. Even so, his deep timbre washed over her, warming her.

"Probably inside this vehicle and on the road to Texas," she said, turning until her back was against the door. She couldn't look at him. Not right then. Because all her defenses would come crashing down around her feet and she couldn't be that vulnerable to him right now.

"Why not right here?" he asked, and his voice was

husky as he trailed his finger along the line of her jaw. He dipped down and kissed her collarbone. A thousand volts shot through her as need welled up, low in her belly.

"Holden," she started but stopped.

"What about here?" He caught her stare for a few seconds and then dipped his head down again. This time, he kissed the spot where her pulse pounded at the base of her neck.

"We shouldn't…"

"Tell me to stop and I will," he said, holding her gaze. There was so much power and promise in that one look from him. This time, she knew better than to seek comfort in his arms. How many times had he pulled away from her every time they got close already?

She tried to form the words but couldn't. She wanted him to keep going until they were lost in each other, in complete bliss and a tangle of arms and legs.

So she looked him dead in the eyes.

"What if I can't?" she asked. "What if I want this?"

Holden swallowed, slicked his tongue across his lips and captured her mouth. He was warm and tasted like the coffee they'd had earlier. Awareness trilled through her at his nearness, at how fast his heart pounded. She brought her hand up to his chest and ran her fingers along the layers of muscle. She smoothed her hand over his masculine pecs.

He captured both of her hands in his, braiding their fingers, and lifted them over her head. Movement thrust her breasts forward and he groaned when the tips of her nipples brushed against him. They beaded and her breasts swelled, needing to be touched. He let go of her right hand and palmed her breast as she arched her back.

Ella opened her eyes and the world tilted when Holden did the same. A bolt of electricity shot through her and she immediately realized that she was in deep trouble.

"Can I keep going?" he asked.

"Yes," she responded without thinking—thinking would have her realize this wouldn't go anywhere. One night sounded amazing and great sex would dim some of the tension pinging between them...

All rational thinking stalled when he brushed his thumb across her nipple and her stomach quivered. Tension corded her muscles, needing relief that only Holden could give.

Ella leaned against the solid vehicle behind her and brought her hands up to Holden's shoulders. Her fingers dug into his shirt as he made her body hum with need by trailing his tongue across her collarbone. Not having sex had never felt so sexy.

His hands cupped her bottom and she wrapped her legs around his toned midsection after he lifted her off her feet. She tunneled her fingers in his hair and his tongue slid in her mouth as his erection pressed into her sex. A familiar force started building inside her body as her tongue roamed freely. She bit his bottom lip as ecstasy pulsed through her. All her senses heightened, her breath started coming out in quick bursts and she could feel that his was, too.

The fact that they were in a garage fully clothed took nothing away from the intimacy and heat of the moment.

"Holden," she managed to say against his mouth, breathless.

"I know." He nipped the conversation in the bud. "This can't go any further."

"Not right now," she said, trying to steady her rapid breathing.

He didn't immediately move and she was grateful.

"This, whatever's happening between us, is moving too fast," she said.

"I know." He surprised her with his response. "We need to take it slow."

"That would be smart," she said, even though her body begged for more.

"We have time to do this the right way," he continued.

A trill of awareness goose bumped her arms and her stomach free-fell. He feathered a kiss on her neck. And then another slow one against her lips. She loved the way he tasted.

"That's the only way I know how to do things," she said. There was so much craziness going on all around them, and yet this was the only thing that made sense to her. She'd never felt this strong of a pull toward another man and that excited and scared her at the same time.

"I could really like you," he said so quietly she almost didn't hear him.

Ella didn't respond. She just stood there with Holden for countless minutes, letting the world stop for just one moment. She wasn't grieving or running or scared. And the world had a strange sense of rightness that she'd never felt before.

Without analyzing it, she breathed in the calm feeling that came over her. Then she wrapped her arms around Holden's neck and looked him in the eye. He had that same hunger she felt deep in her stomach and she needed to let go with him. Life was crazy. Tomorrow wasn't guaranteed. They had *this* moment. Right now. Letting it slip through their fingers would be a costly mistake.

Ella pressed up onto her tiptoes and his mouth came crashing down on hers. No words were needed to move things forward. She could feel his body humming with the same awareness and desire rippling through her.

He brought his hand up and cradled her neck, tilting her head back a little as his tongue brushed against the tips of her teeth. She pushed him back long enough to help him out of his shirt and a few seconds later hers joined his on the floor.

Holden pressed his lips to hers as he cupped her breasts and groaned. "You're beautiful."

"So are you," she said against his mouth.

His hands wrapped around her back, unsnapped her bra and then it joined the shirts on the floor.

Her chest rose and fell quickly as tension heightened her nerves with anticipation. She brought her hands to the waistband of his jeans and tugged at the zipper. He helped her take his off and then her jogging shorts and panties flew to the floor.

She pulled his masculine body against her, her back against the SUV. His erection pulsed against her stomach and she wrapped her legs around his midsection as he lifted her. He eased her down on his full shaft, dipping the head inside and groaned with pleasure when he discovered that she was ready for him. She wiggled her hips until she could take in his full length.

"Holden," she whispered, tangling her fingers in his thick, wavy hair. The feeling of her naked skin against his brought on a wave of ecstasy and anticipation.

He drove himself inside her, his hands on either side of her hips as his mouth found hers.

She said his name again and he thrust deeper in response. Her entire body hummed with need as all her emotions heightened. She matched his thrust this time and then the next. Faster. Harder. Deeper. Until her entire body begged for release. His hands caressed her bottom as he drove inside her until she tipped over the edge of the precipice and free-fell as explosions filled her.

"Holden." She breathed his name as she felt him reach the peak. His muscles corded with tension as she ground her sex on his erection until he rocketed toward the same release.

She had no idea how long he stood holding her in the garage before he finally opened his eyes.

"Ella." Hearing her name spoken softly into her ear was the sweetest sound coming from him.

As her breathing returned to normal, Holden pressed his forehead to hers. He didn't immediately move away and she liked that he didn't. His hands cupped her neck and hers had dropped to his waist. It felt so right to stand there with him in the quiet.

Neither spoke as he eased her to her feet. Neither had to. The silence was comforting. He picked up her clothes first and she admired his glorious body for another few seconds before he dressed.

He gazed at her with a look of appreciation as she dressed and it felt like the most natural thing to be naked with Holden, another foreign feeling.

Once they were dressed, he palmed the keys. He clicked the button to unlock the door and then opened her side first.

Life was short and all her careful planning felt

stifling now. Being with him made her feel alive. At first, she'd chalked it up to adrenaline rushes and danger. But it was Holden. What was so wrong with taking it a step further? Of completely letting go and being with this man in every sense of the words?

One word came to mind. *Love.*

Ella had fallen down that slope and risked her heart being shattered. Sure, she'd been with other men, but she'd never felt this deep of a connection during sex than she did with Holden. Mind-altering, heart-all-in sex.

And when he walked away, her heart would be shattered into a million tiny pieces and scattered across the ranch. She'd already lost her father. While this was no comparison, she couldn't risk losing anyone else. There wouldn't be enough pieces of her to pick up.

Their temporary shelter against the world was about to disappear. She knew full well that they couldn't stay there forever. And yet a piece of her heart wanted exactly that, to hide out with Holden until the rest of the world forgot about both of them, to stay in each other's arms, found instead of lost in the world.

"Ready?" he asked, turning the key in the ignition.

"As much as I'll ever be," she responded.

"Let's see what kind of trouble we can get ourselves

into," he said with a wink and a smile that unleashed a thousand butterflies in her stomach.

Ella, who never let anyone break inside her walls, was in serious trouble.

Chapter Sixteen

The highway stretched on for miles. Ella had finally fallen asleep in the passenger seat. And Holden tried to ignore the ache in his chest. He'd stepped in where he had no business going earlier. Caring about her more wasn't going to help their...*situation*, for lack of a better word, one bit.

The physical attraction pinging between them was one thing. This was another. It was so much deeper than that. The air had changed between them after sex and he needed to protect her more than he needed to breathe. The problem was that nothing had changed. Being seen with him was still a death sentence. He had to figure out a way to give her back her life. He'd bring justice to the men who'd killed his loved ones. Holden was alive again for the first time in two years and his anger bubbled to the surface—anger that had been at a steady simmer since he'd walked inside his house and seen that lifeless body.

And he had a problem because his feelings for

Ella were out of control. He needed to bring them back down to earth because they were dangerous for her. It didn't matter the pain it would cause him; he had to push her away for her own sake.

Could he, though?

Holden watched as cars zipped around him. Morning light was close and there was a motel off the highway where they could get a couple of hours of shut-eye. He grabbed a room key and walked her inside.

The place had two full-size beds and a decent shower, so they could clean up and get a nice meal not far from there. Holden had made this drive on his motorcycle more than once over the years. A piece of him felt contentment with Ella that he'd never experienced before. Leaving her was going to hurt like hell.

"You shower first," he said.

"Okay." She blinked her eyes up at him and he'd be damned but he kissed her.

Holden palmed his father's favorite baseball card as he waited for Ella to finish her shower. When this was all over, he would circle back to Rose. One way or another, this would end. Ella made him see that he'd stopped living, stopped caring. The only thing that had been keeping him alive was his promise to his father and the fact that Rose needed him.

He flipped the card around his fingers, frustrated that he was missing something. His father had been obsessed with Hank Aaron and then Rose had passed along the message 1-9-6-4, which could be a combination or address.

Holden studied the card.

"What are you thinking about so intensely?" Ella asked, and he hadn't even realized she'd turned off the water.

"I'm missing something." He sighed sharply. "What does 1-9-6-4 mean?"

"A home address?" she asked.

"I thought about that, too. Seems like I would remember something and that could be anywhere." He held up the card and flipped it around his fingers. Staring at the back, he said, "1-9-6-4 could be 1964, as in the year."

Hank Aaron's batting average in 1964 was 340.

"What does 340 mean?" she asked.

He pulled the strongbox from his duffel and set it on the bed in between them. She looked up at him and it seemed to dawn on her.

"The combination." Holden punched in the numbers and the box cracked open. He thumbed through ledgers, pages and pages of documented illegal activity. His father was involved in illegal activity?

"Pop got himself into trouble," he said. From what Holden could tell, his father was being forced to use his interstate moving company to move other things. "And the Hampshire Police Chief is involved."

Ella touched his shoulder.

"They were after Pop all along," he said, and it

was like a balloon in his chest had deflated when he exhaled.

"Why? Seems like he was cooperating." Ella studied the documents over his shoulder.

An envelope fell out of the papers with Holden's name on it.

He ripped it open. The note from his father read "If you're reading this, things must've gotten bad. Chief Mallory approached me a year ago with an offer he said I couldn't refuse. He wasn't kidding and made it clear. I cooperated. At first, it was small stuff, a little bit of narcotics and weapons. It grew fast. Then one of my drivers disappeared with a shipment. Forgive me? Love, Pop."

"They must've tried to get to him through you," Ella said.

"All this time I thought it was my fault. I thought I did something to cause the deaths that followed me. I thought I was responsible for Pop being killed." Holden fisted the paper. A mix of sadness and anger and a little bit of hope that this could end filled him.

"I bet the people who showed up at your place that morning thought they would find you, wanting to use you against your father." Ella sat back on her knees. "Karen was in the wrong place at the wrong time."

"That cost her her life, which is something I take seriously."

Ella nodded. "The cop tried to kill you. The police chief must've believed you knew or were in on it somehow."

"And then I went into hiding and they couldn't track me. They tortured and killed Pop because they believed he was involved in that shipment disappearing," he said, anger filled him. "I wish I'd known what Pop had gotten involved in."

"Your dad must've realized how deadly this information could be," she said. "He was trying to protect you."

Holden no longer cared what happened to him. He had to bring the chief to justice for his father and Karen's sakes. Otherwise, their deaths meant nothing. "There was a young attorney general who'd been trying to make a case against the chief for something. I can't remember what exactly. I don't even know if he's still after the chief, but I need to turn this information over to him."

"First, we'll call. Make sure he knows this is coming from you and that you are in no way involved," she said. "And then we'll FedEx the documents. This is all the proof he'll need to bring the chief to justice."

"I don't want to wait. We can stop off on the way to Cattle Barge to send these," he said.

"We'll make a copy. Just in case," she said.

"Let's get out of here." Holden dared to imagine a normal life again. Friday night date nights and a cold beer while watching a game. It had been out of reach for so long that it seemed foreign now. Like all that was a lifetime ago, similar to when he'd returned from overseas after three tours.

And it was still at arm's length. Because he was still wanted for murder.

THE MOTEL ROOM was wiped down and empty inside of twenty minutes. Tension radiated from Holden as he took the wheel of the SUV.

"It's going to work out," Ella reassured, noticing the white-knuckle grip Holden had on the steering wheel.

"What if they've gotten to the attorney general?" He started the engine and navigated out of the pay-by-the-night motel parking lot. "He may want to strike a deal instead of clearing my name."

"He won't," she reassured. "We have definitive proof that you weren't involved and if the attorney general doesn't want to do the right thing, we'll go to the media."

Holden nodded and she was satisfied that he believed her.

"I wish Pop would've told me before. I could've prevented his death." He pulled onto the highway.

"And involve you even more?" she asked. "He loved you too much for that. You would've taken this up for him and he knew it. You would've ended up dead and he wouldn't have been able to live with himself."

"I had a chance. I could've gotten to him sooner,"

he said, and she could see the torment he was putting himself through.

"You have to accept the fact that even though you're a grown man capable of defending yourself and everyone else around you, your father is still your father. If he's anything like you, and I'm guessing the apple didn't fall far from the tree, then he would rather trade his life if it meant saving yours. Besides, he probably blamed himself for not figuring a way out of this sooner."

Holden paused thoughtfully. He focused on the patch of road ahead with a nod.

"I just wish he hadn't been so stubborn," he said. "I could've kept him alive."

"I'm sorry, Holden. I really am. Fathers are hardwired to protect their children no matter how old we are. Yours sounds like a good man, an honest man until his back was against the wall. He didn't deserve what happened to him. And neither did you." She twirled a pen in between her fingers.

Holden gave her a look of appreciation.

"There was no way I could've hurt Karen. I hope the attorney general will be able to see it. I wasn't even there when it happened," he said.

"The attorney general won't overlook that fact," she reassured.

"I hope you're right because you know what the implication is if you're wrong," he said.

She did know. It meant that they were about to

turn over the only true evidence in the case, the only evidence that could clear Holden. "We'll make a copy and keep the original. We'll threaten to use the media if he doesn't cooperate. It'll work out."

"I wish I had your optimism."

Morning traffic was thickening as the sun rose.

Ella sipped the coffee that he'd bought from the mini-mart. It tasted burned in comparison to the stuff Holden made over nothing but a few fire logs, but the caffeine would do the trick. "This attorney general person, is he legitimate?"

"I believe so," he said.

"First impressions are usually right." Even when he had a beard covering his face and hadn't spoken to a person in almost two years, Ella had known that there was something still good about Holden. She was intuitive enough to realize that he was holding something in, too.

His demeanor had changed like it did every time their defenses started tumbling down. It never lasted long and she could see that he was still holding on to the past. He'd never be able to move into the future— a future that she was beginning to hope that the two of them could spend getting to know each other better— if he couldn't let go of the past.

"I guess." He shrugged, keeping his focus on the stretch of highway in front of them. "We'll stop off along Interstate 40 to give the impression we're heading west. It'll add time to our trip but it'll be worth it. In case."

Holden didn't finish. The rest of that sentence involved what would happen if the attorney general didn't believe him. And they both knew what that meant. She could eventually go home but he would have to disappear. Again.

THE CALL WITH the attorney general, Calvin Edwards, had gone better than expected. Holden had tilted the phone so that Ella could hear. He'd said he wanted her perspective. She'd had a good feeling when they ended the conversation.

An hour later, they stopped off at a mailing center.

"This will give Edwards everything he needs to go after them," Holden said to Ella under his breath at the copy company's business center. He placed the package inside the small mailing box and sealed it at the self-check counter. "If it makes it."

"It will," she urged. "Make sure to get a signature."

"And receive confirmation where?" he asked.

She thought about it for a moment. "My email should be fine."

"No way," he said.

"Why not?" she asked. "It's perfect. You don't have one and no one involved would connect me to your father's case."

Holden conceded. He punched in the mix of

letters and numbers as she spoke. He printed the mailing label and placed it on the small box before taking to the cashier.

"Two years is a long time." Holden leaned down and brushed a kiss on her lips after taking a deep breath.

"The timing of this is perfect," she said. "Everyone involved has moved on. No one is expecting evidence to show up now. It'll come out of the blue. You stay under the radar a few more weeks, like Edwards said, and the key players will already be in jail."

As they walked out, Holden fished his cell out of his pocket and held it flat on his palm. "Your turn."

"Sheriff Sawmill, this is Ella Butler," Ella said into the phone after dialing a number.

"I have good news for you, Miss Ella," Sheriff Sawmill said. "We have Suffolk's son in custody."

"Why? What happened?" She tilted the phone so that Holden could hear.

"The shell casings on his father's shotgun matched those at the crime scene. When we hauled his father in, he did the right thing and stepped forward," he said. "Suffolk's gun wasn't stolen and his son took it right from inside the back door."

Ella looked at Holden, searching for something that she wasn't sure could exist so early in their relationship.

"It's over, Miss Ella. We got him. Handcuffed

him this morning," he said. "It's safe for you to come home."

"He's responsible for both attacks? For the rock at Devil's Lid?" she asked. Tears brimmed at that last word because without her father she wondered if Hereford would still feel like home. What would it be now? An odd feeling settled in her chest. Nothing felt the same anymore, nor had it since her father's death, and she doubted it ever would again. And she had to wonder how much the man standing next to her influenced that.

"We believe so," Sawmill supplied.

"Thank you, Sheriff," Ella said.

"I didn't want to release a statement to the media until I delivered the message to you personally," he said. "They're outside now."

It would be all over the news soon.

"I appreciate it," she said. "Can you give me five minutes to tell my family that I'm okay?"

"You bet," Sheriff Sawmill said.

The two exchanged goodbyes and she made a quick call to May, who promised to let the others know immediately.

"Everyone's fine, other than my sister having the flu. It's over. And I should feel more relieved," Ella said to Holden.

"Do you think they have the wrong guy?" he asked.

"I wouldn't say that exactly. I'm not sure what's

wrong." She couldn't pinpoint what was going on in her mind. "It's probably just me. I'm off. This whole experience has been surreal and it's just hard to believe that it's all over. Everything feels different about the ranch now. The second I start to feel relief about going home I realize that my dad's not going to be there. Suddenly, Hereford doesn't feel as much like home as it used to."

Holden took her in his arms and she buried her face in his strong chest. Those strong arms of his wrapped around her and she couldn't deny that this felt like home.

"Will you come back with me?" She blinked away tears and looked up at him.

"I should check on Rose," he said before pressing a kiss to her forehead.

"We could send for her. She hasn't been away in a while and she might enjoy being on the ranch for a few days." Ella wasn't sure if she'd convinced him but Rose was always welcome at Hereford.

Holden stood there for a long moment. Ella pressed up to her tiptoes and placed her hands on his shoulders. She looked into his eyes before kissing him. There was no hesitation in his reaction, his lips pressed to her and his tongue tasting her.

Ella pulled back first and looked into his intense blue eyes. "Can you give me a few more days?"

His face broke into a smile as he trailed his finger

along her cheek. "You can be convincing when you set your mind to something, can't you?"

"Only when it's the right thing to do," she countered, matching his smile. "Does that mean you'll stay?"

"Yes."

She wrapped her arms around his neck and rewarded him with another kiss. Happiness lifted the weight from her shoulders. They were going home. Even if Hereford was a temporary stop for Holden.

Chapter Seventeen

Being back in Cattle Barge reminded Ella of what a media circus the town had become. A hot shower, May's cooking and Holden nearby would go a long way toward making her feel like she could deal with it all again.

Of course, she would feel better if she could access the memory buzzing around in the back of her thoughts. Trying to force it threatened to split her head open. "Remind me to take a couple of ibuprofen the minute we get to Hereford."

Even with the pain, her excitement was building.

"We have some." Holden kept one hand firmly on the wheel and the other reached around and retrieved the duffel.

"I forgot all about these," she said. They'd been on the road twelve hours steady aside from a pair of bathroom breaks since leaving the motel. Ten was pretty much her limit. Even in the comfortable SUV, the ride dragged on and it was probably because she missed being home so much.

"Are you hungry?" Holden asked.

"I can make it. Another forty minutes and we're there." She was already thinking about May's cooking, the kitchen. The place was an old-world farmhouse with the oversize single sink, and had white cabinets and granite countertops. There was a hand-carved wooden table in the kitchen that stretched almost end to end. One side was used for food prep and the rest of the table was used for eating. She couldn't wait to show Holden around the main house.

To avoid traffic, she'd directed Holden to a back road. There was no way she wanted to face the media. Not now. All she wanted to do was get home and call her brothers. She wanted to check on her younger sister, Cadence, to see if she was recovering from the flu she'd caught as everything was going down about their father. Cadence rarely ever got sick and stress had most likely weakened her immune system.

"Feeling better?" Holden asked a few minutes later.

"They're starting to kick in." Thank the stars for pain relievers.

"Are you worried about being home again?"

"Not as much as I thought I would be," she admitted, and it had everything to do with the man sitting next to her. The feeling of missing her dad wasn't going away anytime soon, but she felt ready to face the fact that he was gone, and that was a huge step for her.

Ella leaned her head back. A comfortable silence sat between them as Holden navigated the country road and she waited for the last of her headache to ease. She checked the time. They were ten minutes from home now and Ella's excitement only increased now that she was so close to Hereford.

Out of nowhere, the sound of a bullet split the air and the SUV spun a hard right. Ella gasped as the vehicle rammed into a tree. Airbags deployed. The next thing she knew she heard a door open and saw Holden being dragged out of the driver's seat.

It took a second to register that he wasn't fighting back. Was he conscious?

Ella tried to work her seat belt but it wouldn't budge and her fingers were so shaky. Panic seized her lungs as she tried to climb out anyway. How had the man gotten Holden out so quickly? She craned her neck to the left and then to the right but couldn't find him. "Holden."

The fact that there was no response chilled her to the bone.

"Holden," she shouted, louder this time.

A hand wrapped around her mouth. She tried to bite the fingers. Failed.

"You just won't die," the masculine voice said. And she absolutely knew that this man was there for her. Because that memory she'd been trying to reach came crashing down around her at the sound of his voice. He'd shouted for her to stop when she'd taken off running. He was the man who was trying to kill her, Troy Alderant. He was the developer who'd tried to buy Suffolk's land.

Old Man Suffolk's son was in jail. He'd confessed. Why would an innocent man confess to a crime he didn't commit? All the details of the conversation she'd had with the sheriff jammed in her brain. Nothing made sense. Except from somewhere deep down she knew this was the man Sheriff Sawmill should be looking for.

She was jerked out of the passenger seat and then thrown onto the unforgiving dirt. Her hands were rammed behind her back and tied. She struggled, kicking and screaming.

But Alderant was strong. Too strong.

"Holden," she shouted out of panic and desperation.

She rolled over in time to see a leering face coming toward her. "Why are you doing this?"

"You and your little pet projects. You couldn't leave well enough alone, could you?" he mumbled. "You don't have my vision for Cattle Barge and that's your problem. Donating more land for animals instead of taking advantage of the lake as a destination is beyond me."

What was he talking about? He'd been around

the past year or so, trying to get involved in local politics. Was he trying to develop the land for something? He must've had his eye on Suffolk's land and the surrounding area.

And she'd accidently gotten in his way.

"We were coming to terms until you ruined it," Alderant said, dragging her by her feet behind the SUV.

If he'd put his plans out in the public too early, residents would've denied it. People had been trying to develop the lake for as long as Ella could remember. Proposals were always being shot down in town hall meetings. This guy must've figured if he bought up enough of the land, he'd have more voting rights. Once he hit the tipping point he could make his plans known and no one would be able to block him.

Ella gasped. Could he be responsible for her father's murder? "Why'd you kill my father? Did he find out about your plans?"

A strangled noise tore from his throat. "I didn't. Your father's death was the best thing that ever happened to me. He was always in Suffolk's ear and the old man wouldn't have sold his land without Butler's approval. I wish I'd thought of killing him. I seized the moment, figuring if I got rid of you I'd be set. Your siblings don't share your passion for animals. No one would've been left to block me. I'd followed you for days when you took that walk on Devil's Lid. I saw my chance to make this go away, to make *you* go away and to keep my name out of it. Everyone would assume your father's killer had set his sights on you."

Ella kicked harder as she realized the other end of the line that tied her hands together was being secured around the back of the SUV.

"But there was a confession," she said.

"To keep his old man out of jail, I presume." The icy voice sent chills down her spine. "You can fight all you want. This time, you die."

A figure launched toward Alderant. Holden?

The two went down in a tangle of fists.

"Grab the phone, call 9-1-1 and get out of here," Holden shouted to Ella.

She used the SUV as balance to get to her feet. Her hands were still tied together behind her back and she needed something to cut the tie. Her pulse raced as she moved toward the open door of the SUV and raked the corner between her hands. Her wrists hurt like hell but adrenaline dulled the pain.

It felt like it took forever to break free from her bindings. She immediately located the cell and called 9-1-1, as instructed, keeping one eye on the fight going on a few yards away from her. The two were on their feet now as she relayed details of their location to the dispatcher.

Holden slammed his fist into Alderant's face. His head snapped backward. The two struggled for something. *A weapon?* And she watched in horror as a metal blade was driven into Holden.

Ella screamed and Alderant glanced toward her, giving Holden the second he needed to regain the upper hand. Holden took the knife, tossed it far away and landed a punch so hard Alderant fell backward.

In a beat, Holden was straddled over Alderant, pounding him until he went still. And then Holden dropped, too.

"Holden." Panicked, Ella ran to him as he lay splayed out on his back. He looked like a doll someone had tossed onto the floor in a hurry and then left behind. His legs were bent and twisted at odd angles. There was blood everywhere, soaking his shirt and jeans. She couldn't even allow herself to think that anything had happened to him as she dropped down beside him. Her lungs felt like they would collapse and her throat closed up. Her chest seized as she saw him there, helpless. He'd taken that knife for her.

Ella folded forward next to his ear. His eyes were closed and he didn't move. Was he breathing? Panic squeezed her chest, making it almost impossible to take in air as she heard the faint sounds of sirens in the night air.

"Breathe," she said in his ear, fighting against the wall of emotions threatening to break down and come crashing around her. She searched for a pulse on his wrist, any sign to tell her that he was still alive.

And then his eyes blinked open. Those gorgeous blue eyes of his. Tears streaked her cheeks.

"I love you," she whispered into his ear. "Stay with me. Please."

His eyes closed as the cavalry arrived.

"Help us, please," she said to the first officer on the scene. "That man caused us to wreck and stabbed my boyfriend."

Alderant was still knocked out cold as he was cuffed. He was going to jail for the rest of his life.

At least for Ella, justice would be served. As for her father, she was resolved to help the sheriff find the person responsible.

THE RIDE TO the hospital in the sheriff's SUV seemed to take forever. Once there, the coffee tasted watered-down but she was grateful for the caffeine boost after she'd downed several cups. There never was much else to do in a hospital while waiting on a loved one than drink cup after cup. She'd paced the halls the entire night even though the doctor had visited with her hours ago and said that Holden would be okay. She'd asked to see him but the doctor asked her to wait until Holden woke. That was four hours ago.

"Ma'am?" a female voice said, startling Ella out of her thoughts.

"Yes."

"You can go in now," the nurse wearing the name tag Roberta said.

"Thank you." Ella didn't waste time turning down the hall and rushing past the nurses' station. She already knew Holden was in room 132. She pushed open the door, scared of what condition she might find him in.

"Finally, the view is worth looking at in here," he said with a smile that reminded her of the fact he was on pretty good pain medication.

"Holden." She rushed to his side and took his hand. "How do you feel?"

"Better now."

She eased onto the side of the bed, afraid she'd hurt him if she moved too fast.

"You can't hurt me," he said with the smile that was so good at breaking down her walls.

"Doctor says you're going to be fine." She looked into those blue eyes of his. Those gorgeous blue eyes.

"He'll let me out later today if everything goes well," he said.

"Is that a good idea?" Panic gripped her.

"Yeah. I want to be with you."

"I'll stay here," she offered.

"It's not a bad injury. I'll be fine by dinner. And there's something I need to say that can't wait."

Ella tensed, afraid he was about to drop the bomb that it was time the two of them parted ways. Her heart would shred but she forced a game face.

"Life without you isn't living, Ella. I'm all in. I'm in love with you and I'd be the happiest man on earth if you would do me the honor of marrying me. I know it's early and we haven't had a long time to get to know each other. But I feel like I've known you all my life. I've made a lot of mistakes but this is a choice I feel good about. The choice I'm making is *you*."

Ella dared to hope this could be real because she felt it just as strongly. "Are you sure this isn't the medication talking?"

"Not a chance. I want to spend the rest of my life with you, but I'll wait until you're sure."

"I don't need time. I need you. Yes, I'll be your wife." Ella wiped away joyful tears streaming down her cheeks. "I fell in love with you the second I looked into your eyes and saw what kind of man you really are, the one I want to spend the rest of my life getting to know even better."

"I love you, Ella," Holden said as he looked up at her. There was so much love in those blue eyes. "I'm done drifting. You're my home."

A WAVE OF gratitude washed over Ella as she woke from a good night's sleep in her own bed for the second time since Alderant's arrest. The other side was empty, so Holden must already be up. The doctor wouldn't be thrilled but she had a feeling that Holden had a good handle on what was best for him while he recovered.

Besides, knowing him, he was probably making

a cup of coffee for May. Lucky her. Ella was more than pleased that two of the most important people in her life got along so well. Her brothers would most likely be more critical, protective instinct being what it was, but Holden was exactly the kind of guy they'd hang out with. And soon the two of them would be married. Her brothers would never argue against a man who made her this happy.

Ella stretched and pushed off the covers. She could use caffeine and a pair of pain relievers.

The news had broken last night about the scandal involving the chief of police. Apparently, the attorney general had wanted to act fast before word leaked of the kind of evidence in his possession. The internet couldn't get enough of replaying a police chief in handcuffs. Holden would finally see justice served for his father and Karen. And when he'd gone to bed last night, it was as if a weight had been lifted.

Ella moved to the dresser to find a pair of jogging pants to throw on so she could find her fiancé. Rose would be flying in later today and Ella couldn't wait for her to see Hereford.

A folded piece of paper caused Ella to freeze. She'd forgotten about the note her father had left there before his death. She picked it up, thinking that his hands had touched the same places not so long ago. Ella pressed the paper to her chest and forced back the tears threatening.

She opened the paper and read the words.

You haven't hiked Devil's Lid since you were little. A trip there might just help you find where you belong.

—D

Ella's heart fisted and tears streamed down her cheeks as she realized that her father had been trying to lead her to Holden. That, even now, she felt like her father was looking out for her.

And even though he was gone, she knew in her heart that he would always watch over her.

* * * * *

Look for more books in USA TODAY
bestselling author Barb Han's
CRISIS: CATTLE BARGE *miniseries,*
coming soon.

And don't miss the titles in her
previous miniseries,
CATTLEMEN CRIME CLUB:

STOCKYARD SNATCHING
DELIVERING JUSTICE
ONE TOUGH TEXAN
TEXAS-SIZED TROUBLE
TEXAS WITNESS
TEXAS SHOWDOWN

Available now from Harlequin Intrigue!

SPECIAL EXCERPT FROM

Tucker Cahill returns to Gilt Edge, Montana, with no choice but to face down his haunted past when a woman's skeletal remains are found near his family's ranch—but he couldn't have prepared for a young woman seeking vengeance and finding much more.

Read on for a sneak preview of
HERO'S RETURN,
A CAHILL RANCH NOVEL
from New York Times *bestselling author*
B.J. Daniels!

Skeletal Remains Found in Creek

The skeletal remains of a woman believed to be in her late teens or early twenties were discovered in Miner's Creek outside of Gilt Edge, Montana, yesterday. Local coroner Sonny Bates estimated that the remains had been in the creek for somewhere around twenty years.

Sheriff Flint Cahill is looking into missing-persons cases from that time in the hopes of identifying the victim. If anyone has any information, they are encouraged to call the Gilt Edge Sheriff's Department.

"No, MRS. KERN, I can assure you that the bones that were found in the creek are not those of your nephew Billy," Sheriff Flint Cahill said into the phone at his desk. "I saw Billy last week at the casino. He was alive and well…No, it takes longer than a week for a body to decompose to nothing but bones. Also, the skeletal remains that were found were a young woman's…Yes, Coroner Sonny Bates can tell the difference."

He looked up as the door opened and his sister, Lillie, stepped into his office. From the scowl on her face, he didn't have to ask what kind of mood she was in. He'd been expecting her, given that he had their father locked up in one of the cells.

"Mrs. Kern, I have to go. I'm sorry Billy hasn't called you, but I'm sure he's fine." He hung up with a sigh. "Dad's in the back sleeping it off. Before he passed out, he mumbled about getting back to the mountains."

A very pregnant Lillie nodded but said nothing. Pregnancy had made his sister even prettier. Her long dark hair framed a face that could only be called adorable. This morning, though, he saw something in her gray eyes that worried him.

He waited for her to tie into him, knowing how she felt about him arresting their father for being drunk and disorderly. This wasn't their first rodeo. And like always, it was Lillie who came to bail Ely out—not his bachelor brothers, Hawk and Cyrus, who wanted to avoid one of Flint's lectures.

He'd been telling his siblings that they needed to do something about their father. But no one wanted to face the day when their aging dad couldn't continue to spend most of his life in the mountains gold panning and trapping—let alone get a snoot full of booze every time he finally hit town again.

"I'll go get him," Flint said, lumbering to his feet. Since he'd gotten the call about the bones being found at the creek, he hadn't had but a few hours' sleep. All morning, the phone had been ringing off the hook. Not with leads on the identity of the skeletal remains—just residents either being nosy or worried there was a killer on the loose.

"Before you get Dad..." Lillie seemed to hesitate, which wasn't like her. She normally spoke her mind without any encouragement at all.

He braced himself.

"A package came for Tuck."

That was the last thing Flint had expected out of her mouth. "To the saloon?"

"To the ranch. No return address."

Flint felt his heart begin to pound harder. It was the first news of their older brother, Tucker, since he'd left home right after high school. Being the second oldest, Flint had been closer to Tucker than with his younger brothers. For years, he'd feared him dead. When Tuck had left like that, Flint had suspected his brother was in some kind of trouble. He'd been sure of it. But had it been something bad enough that Tucker hadn't felt he could come to Flint for help?

"Did you open the package?" he asked.

Lillie shook her head. "Hawk and Cyrus thought about it but then called me."

He tried to hide his irritation that one of them had called their sister instead of him, the darned sheriff. His brothers had taken over the family ranch and were the only ones still living on the property, so it wasn't a surprise that they would have received the package. Which meant that whoever had sent it either didn't know that Tucker no longer lived there or thought he was coming back for some reason.

Because Tucker was on his way home? Maybe he'd sent the package and there was nothing to worry about.

Unfortunately, a package after all this time didn't necessarily bode well. At least not to Flint, who came by his suspicious nature naturally as a lawman. He feared it might be Tucker's last effects.

"I hope *you* didn't open it."

Lillie shook her head. "You think this means he's coming home?" She sounded so hopeful it made his heart ache. He and Tucker had been close in more ways than age. Or at least he'd thought so. But something had been going on with his brother his senior year in high school and Flint had no idea what it was. Or if trouble was still dogging his brother.

For months after Tucker left, Flint had waited for him to return. He'd been so sure that whatever the trouble was, it was temporary. But after all these years, he'd given up any hope. He'd feared he would never see his brother again.

"Tell them not to open it. I'll stop by the ranch and check it out."

Lillie met his gaze. "It's out in my SUV. I brought it with me."

Flint swore under his breath. What if it had a bomb in it? He knew that was overly dramatic, but still, knowing his sister... There wasn't a birthday or Christmas present that she hadn't shaken the life out of as she'd tried to figure out what was inside it. "Is your truck open?" She nodded. "Wait here."

He stepped out into the bright spring day. Gilt Edge sat in a saddle surrounded by four mountain ranges still tipped with snow. Picturesque, tourists came here to fish its blue-ribbon trout stream. But winters were long and a town of any size was a long way off.

Sitting in the middle of Montana, Gilt Edge also had something that most tourists didn't see. It was surrounded by underground missile silos. The one on the Cahill Ranch was renowned because that was where their father swore he'd seen a UFO not only land, but also that he'd been forced on board back in 1967. Which had made their father the local crackpot.

Flint took a deep breath, telling himself to relax. His life was going well. He was married to the love of his life. But still, he felt a foreboding that he couldn't shake off. A package for Tucker after all these years?

The air this early in the morning was still cold, but there was a scent to it that promised spring wasn't that far off. He loved spring and summers here and had been looking forward to picnics, trail rides and finishing the yard around the house he and Maggie were building.

He realized that he'd been on edge since he'd gotten the call about the human bones found in the creek. Now he could admit it. He'd felt as if he was waiting for the other shoe to drop. And now this, he thought as he stepped to his sister's SUV.

The box sitting in the passenger-side seat looked battered. He opened the door and hesitated for a moment before picking it up. For its size, a foot-and-a-half-sized cube, the package was surprisingly light. As he lifted the box out, something shifted inside. The sound wasn't a rattle. It was more a rustle like dead leaves followed by a slight thump.

Like his sister had said, there was no return address. Tucker's name and the ranch address had been neatly printed in black—not in his brother's handwriting. The generic cardboard box was battered enough to suggest it had come from a great distance, but that wasn't necessarily true. It could have looked like that when the sender found it discarded and decided to use it to send the contents. He hesitated for a moment, feeling foolish. But he heard nothing ticking inside. Closing the SUV door, he carried the box inside and put it behind his desk.

"Aren't you going to open it?" Lilly asked, wide-eyed.

"No. You need to take Dad home." He started past his sister but vacillated. "I wouldn't say anything to him about this. We don't want to get his hopes up that Tucker might be headed home. Or make him worry."

She glanced at the box and nodded. "Did you ever understand why Tuck left?"

Flint shook his head. He was torn between anger and sadness when it came to his brother. Also fear. What had happened Tucker's senior year in high school? What if the answer was in that box?

"By the way," he said to his sister, "I didn't arrest Dad. Ely voluntarily turned himself in last night." He shrugged. Flint had never understood his father any more than he had his brother Tuck. To this day, Ely swore that he had been out by the missile silo buried in the middle of their ranch when a UFO landed, took him aboard and did experiments on him.

Then again, their father liked his whiskey and always had.

"You all right?" he asked his sister when she still said nothing.

Lillie nodded distractedly and placed both hands over the baby growing inside her. She was due any day now. He hoped the package for Tucker wasn't something that would hurt his family. He didn't want anything upsetting his sister in her condition. But he could see that just the arrival of the mysterious box had Lillie worried. She wasn't the only one.

TUCKER CAHILL SLOWED his pickup as he drove through Gilt Edge. He'd known it would be emotional, returning after all these years. He'd never doubted he would return—he just hadn't expected it to take nineteen years. All that time, he'd been waiting like a man on death row, knowing how it would eventually end.

Still, he was filled with a crush of emotion. *Home.* He hadn't realized how much he'd missed it, how much he'd missed his family, how much he'd missed his life in Montana. He'd been waiting for this day, dreading it and, at the same time, anxious to return at least once more.

As he started to pull into a parking place in front of the sheriff's department, he saw a pregnant woman come out followed by an old man with long gray hair and a beard. His breath caught. Not sure if he was more shocked to see how his father had aged—or how pregnant and grown up his little sister, Lillie, was now.

He couldn't believe it as he watched Lillie awkwardly climb into an SUV, the old man going around to the passenger side. He felt his heart swell at the sight of them. Lillie had been nine when he'd left.

But he could never forget a face that adorable. Was that really his father? He couldn't believe it. When had Ely Cahill become an old mountain man?

He wanted to call out to them but stopped himself. As much as he couldn't wait to see them, there was something he had to take care of first. Tears burned his eyes as he watched Lillie drive their father away. It appeared he was about to be an uncle. Over the years while he was hiding out, he'd made a point of following what news he could from Gilt Edge. He'd missed so much with his family.

He swallowed the lump in his throat as he opened his pickup door and stepped out. The good news was that his brother Flint was sheriff. That, he hoped, would make it easier to do what he had to do. But facing Flint after all this time away... He knew he owed his family an explanation, but Flint more than the rest. He and his brother had been so close—until his senior year.

He braced himself as he pulled open the door to the sheriff's department and stepped in. He'd let everyone down nineteen years ago, Flint especially. He doubted his brother would have forgotten—or forgiven him.

But that was the least of it, Flint would soon learn.

AFTER HIS SISTER LEFT, Flint moved the battered cardboard box to the corner of his desk. He'd just pulled out his pocketknife to cut through the tape when his intercom buzzed.

"There's a man here to see you," the dispatcher said. He could hear the hesitation in her voice. "He says he's your *brother*?" His family members never had the dispatcher announce them. They just came on back to his office. *"Your brother Tucker?"*

Flint froze for a moment. Hands shaking, he laid down his pocketknife as relief surged through him. Tucker was alive and back in Gilt Edge? He had to clear his throat before he said, "Send him in."

He told himself he wasn't prepared for this and yet it was something he'd dreamed of all these years. He stepped around to the front of his desk, half-afraid of what to expect. A lot could have happened to his brother in nineteen years. The big question, though, was why come back now?

As a broad-shouldered cowboy filled his office doorway, Flint blinked. He'd been expecting the worst.

Instead, Tucker looked great. Still undeniably handsome with his thick dark hair and gray eyes like the rest of the Cahills, Tucker had filled out from the teenager who'd left home. Wherever he'd been, he'd apparently fared well. He appeared to have been doing a lot of physical labor, because he was buff and tanned.

Flint was overwhelmed by both love and regret as

he looked at Tuck, and furious with him for making him worry all these years.

"Hello, Flint," Tucker said, his voice deeper than Flint remembered.

He couldn't speak for a moment, afraid of what would come out of his mouth. The last thing he wanted to do was drive his brother away again. He wanted to hug him and slug him at the same time.

Instead, he said, voice breaking, "Tuck. It's so damned good to see you," and closed the distance between them to pull his older brother into a bear hug.

TUCKER HUGGED FLINT, fighting tears. It had been so long. Too long. His heart broke at the thought of the lost years. But Flint looked good, taller than Tucker remembered, broader shouldered, too.

"When did you get so handsome?" Tucker said as he pulled back, his eyes still burning with tears. It surprised him that they were both about the same height. Like him, Flint had filled out. With their dark hair and gray eyes, they could almost pass for twins.

The sheriff laughed. "You know darned well that you're the prettiest of the bunch of us."

Tucker laughed, too, at the old joke. It felt good. Just like it felt good to be with family again. "Looks like you've done all right for yourself."

Flint sobered. "I thought I'd never see you again."

"Like Dad used to say, I'm like a bad penny. I'm

bound to turn up. How is the old man? Was that him I saw leaving with Lillie?"

"You didn't talk to them?" Flint sounded both surprised and concerned.

"I wanted to see you first." Tucker smiled as Flint laid a hand on his shoulder and squeezed gently before letting go.

"You know how he was after Mom died. Now he spends almost all of his time up in the mountains panning gold and trapping. He had a heart attack a while back, but it hasn't slowed him down. There's no talking any sense into him."

"Never was." Tucker nodded as a silence fell between them. He and Flint had once been so close. Regret filled him as Flint studied him for a long moment before he stepped back and motioned him toward a chair in his office.

Closing the door, Flint settled into his chair behind his desk. Tucker dragged up one of the office chairs.

"I wondered if you wouldn't be turning up, since Lillie brought in a package addressed to you when she came to pick up Dad. He often spends a night in my jail when he's in town. Drunk and disorderly."

Tucker didn't react to that. He was looking at the battered brown box sitting on Flint's desk. *"A package?"* His voice broke. No one could have known he was coming back here unless…

Don't miss
HERO'S RETURN,
available March 2018 wherever
HQN Books and ebooks are sold.

www.Harlequin.com

COMING NEXT MONTH FROM
ⓗ HARLEQUIN®

INTRIGUE

Available April 17, 2018

#1779 COWBOY'S REDEMPTION
The Montana Cahills • by B.J. Daniels
Former army pilot Colt McCloud never forgot the woman he rescued over a year ago. Now back home on his Montana ranch, Colt discovers Lola Dayton on his doorstep...and learns that their baby girl has been kidnapped.

#1780 ONE INTREPID SEAL
Mission: Six • by Elle James
After rescuing Reese Brantley in the Congo, can Navy SEAL "Diesel" Dalton Samuel Landon avoid getting them both abducted by warring factions—and at the same time not lose his heart to the beautiful bodyguard?

#1781 FINDING THE EDGE
Colby Agency: Sexi-ER • by Debra Webb
With a target on her back thanks to a vengeful gang leader, nurse Eva Bowman turns to the Colby Agency for protection. Can she trust investigator Todd Christian with her life—even if he once broke her young, vulnerable heart?

#1782 UNDERCOVER SCOUT
Apache Protectors: Wolf Den • by Jenna Kernan
Tribal police detective Ava Hood has every intention of bringing down a surrogacy ring. Then she learns all roads lead to Dr. Kee Redhorse's clinic, and her attraction to the sexy physician becomes a lot more complicated...

#1783 ENDANGERED HEIRESS
Crisis: Cattle Barge • by Barb Han
A heartbreaking loss brings rancher Hudson Dale home to Cattle Barge, where he crosses paths with Madelyn Kensington. Thanks to the terms of a will, the beautiful stranger has become a target, giving Hudson the chance at redemption he desperately craves.

#1784 THE SHERIFF'S SECRET
Protectors of Cade County • by Julie Anne Lindsey
When Tina Ellet's infant daughter is abducted, Sheriff West Garrett vows to save the child, capture the criminal and prove to Tina that their love is worth fighting for.

_____

YOU CAN FIND MORE INFORMATION ON UPCOMING HARLEQUIN® TITLES, FREE EXCERPTS AND MORE AT WWW.HARLEQUIN.COM.

HICNM0418